# Down a Road
# I've Never Been

## by
## Richart Drake Lewis

*To my friends and family in Cicero.
Hope you enjoy this.
Love always
Richart Drake Lewis
"2004"*

**Cork Hill Press**
Indianapolis

CORK HILL PRESS™

Cork Hill Press
7520 East 88th Place, Suite 101
Indianapolis, Indiana 46256-1253
1-866-688-BOOK
www.corkhillpress.com

Issued simultaneously in hardcover and trade paperback editions.
Hardcover Edition: 1-59408-487-4
Trade Paperback Edition: 1-59408-278-2

Library of Congress Card Catalog Number: 2003110703

**Printed in the United States of America**

September 2003

**1 3 5 7 9 10 8 6 4 2**

## DEDICATION

I would like to dedicate this book to the following people...

Roy Miller
My best friend and my brother. You will always be more than those simple words to me.

Carol Anne Oddley
You are the breath of air that will forever blow through the winds of my life.

Jennifer La' Nette Tate
You left such an impression upon my life that I have never forgotten you, or the friends that touched both our lives in the summer of '72. I love you, Jenn. I always have, and I always will...

## ACKNOWLEDGMENTS

A book like this takes a lot of time, a lot memories, a lot of people, and a lot of tears to complete. If not for the characters that shared these events with me in the summer of '72 this story might not have ever been told.

It has lived with me for a very long time, and gone through several drafts before reaching this final one. It's even gone through four different titles.

I first wrote it as a short story in 1992 for one of my ICL classes under the title "The Night Jennifer Tate Died". Judith Enderle, my instructor and writer herself, asked me to flesh the story out and see where I could go with it. It then became a novel titled "The Thinking Rock".

That poor novel went through hell for the next decade. My third wife at the time was jealous of Jenn and the fact that I held her memory so dear. She upset me to the point where I burned all the hard copies of it in a failed attempt to please her. I did, however, keep the disks I had it recorded on, but discovered after my divorce that the disks had mysteriously disappeared from there hiding place. It wasn't surprising considering the fact that my now ex was always rummaging through my personal things (my past) to find new avenues to attack me with.

After the divorce my oldest son and I moved back to Tennessee to get away from the life that had robbed us both of more than we could ever replace, and for reasons I would much rather keep to myself. Once there I tracked down all the key characters in the book and resumed my relationships with them.

Surrounded by all these memories I found myself rewriting the book with a new fever under the title "The Summer of '72". Roy Miller found an add for an agent in Texas who I submitted the first 36 pages to. He agreed to represent my book for a fee, and I soon found myself polishing up the book once more still under the same title.

More than two years later, and not providing the service I had paid for I pulled the book from his service. I put it in a box, moved back to Indiana, and tried to forget I had ever written it.

I didn't count on the book having a life of its own.

After another brother friend of mine (Harvey Johns) expressed interest in it, and found a publisher who might be willing to take it on I pulled it out for another look to see if it would be worth the journey. I contacted the publisher (Sandy Maine at Cork Hill Press), and began a new adventure.

I sat down and started rewriting the book once more (the one found in these pages) under the title "Down a Road I've Never Been". I chose that title because it honestly best fit the path I had taken with everything that eventually made it what it was to me and all those involved with it.

It's written as fiction because I had to omit some of the characters and locals that appear in the truth. This was because I couldn't find some of the characters to get their permission, and without them some of the locations just wouldn't work. Other than that, the story is pretty much in tack, and not hurt by any of the things omitted.

Those that are in the book are very excited that it's finally going to be published, and are waiting to purchase their copies of it. When I told them that I was planning to give them all a copy of it anyway the response was all the same. "If you give away copies of the book, how is it ever going to become a best seller?"

I only pray that the book and I can live up to a measure of the faith these friends have awarded us with. Like my English Comp Professor Douglas Gordon at Austin Peavy University said in one of his classes, "Only time, the right promotion, and the audience will tell of a book's ultimate worth."

That may be true in the literary world, but it leaves out one important piece of the process. The book tells the true worth, and I believe that this one has everything it possibly can have going for it.

If you care to write me about your thoughts on reading it, you can reach me by either writing to the publisher, or by writing to me at:

Richart Drake Lewis
460 North West Street
Tipton, Indiana 46072

I'll be happy to reply to anyone who drops me a line.

# CHAPTER ONE

WOODLAWN SHORES, TENNESSEE, WAS probably the last place in the world I wanted to be during the summer of '72.

In fact I know it was.

I had all these plans for the summer that I wanted to do my best to see through. Plans that I believed would make a big difference in the rest of my life.

One way or another I was going to get Lisa McFall to like me for who I was, and not just think I was a passing phase. The only problem I was having at the moment was the really big fact that she came across like she could care less about who Ryc Lewis was. We had this really weird relationship going on that I can't really explain. I thought she was playing hard to get, and she thought I was this stupid teenager in love.

My best friend, Jerry Young, and I were planning to spend the summer working with his father's roofing business. Our goal was to earn enough money to buy our own set of wheels to drive back and forth to school in the coming year. We had this bad habit of getting kicked off the bus for various reasons, and were getting tired of walking home from wherever the bus driver let us off.

Only that wasn't going to happen.

My Dad moved us from West Elwood, Indiana to Woodlawn Shores, Tennessee, just a week after school had let out for the year. It wasn't my idea, or choice for that matter. I liked where I was just fine, and could careless about the reasons we were moving. My Dad, on the other hand, moved at any given notion.

This was one of those times. Kinda.

"I don't want to move to Tennessee," I said, from the back seat of the car, as we were on our way.

Dad, shot me one of his famous hard looks.

"Right now, you have no other choice in the matter," he stated, which was an understatement.

"Was I even asked?" I said, more to myself, then him.

"I thought you liked it in Tennessee," Mom said. "After all, you did spend last summer down there with your Uncle Pete."

"Moving there isn't the same as spending the summer there," I stated. "It's two very different concepts."

"It's a concept you had better get used to," Dad said. "Besides, we're going to be living in the same house, your uncle lived in."

"Yeah, I know," I said. "He moves into the big town of Parsons, Tennessee, while we get to live out in the middle of nowhere."

"That'll be enough of that, Richart," Dad said, obviously treading the limits of his irritation. "Your uncle got me a job offer I can't refuse at this time. If you know what I mean."

Yeah, I knew what he meant. He and Mom had gotten in way over their heads, buying the little farm we had in West Elwood. Especially, after his employer decided to close the doors, and relocate to Florida. That unfortunately meant that they could no longer make the payments. In the end, it was turned over to my Uncle Coy and Aunt Marie, who had originally co-signed for the loan that got them the farm in the first place.

Oddly enough, it would be Mom and Dad's loss.

"What about my friends?" I asked.

"You'll make new friends," Dad said, without giving any true thought to what I was actually asking him.

"I don't wanna make new friends."

2

"Then I guess you won't have any," he stated, as if it were a matter of fact.

"It's not fair," I protested. "I've spent most of my life making those friends. What are they gonna think about me just leaving without saying anything?"

"Friends come and go like the wind," he replied. "If the ones you leave behind are truly your friends, they'll still be your friends when you see them again."

"What about that girl you talked so much about when you came back from your visit last summer?" Mom asked.

"Carol Anne?" I smiled, at her memory. "I forgot about her being there."

"Don't get too attached to the idea," Dad said. "You're way too young to be thinking about girls."

"She's just a friend, Dad," I said.

"At least you've got a friend," my middle brother Jim stated. "Joe and I don't know anyone in Tennessee."

"Who asked you?" I snapped, wondering what it was to him. He wasn't old enough to worry about friends the way I did.

"We're moving too," my little brother Joe added.

"There will be no fighting," Dad snapped. "We're moving, and that's that. So get used to it, because it's not gonna change."

That's how I ended up in Tennessee. It didn't matter that I was born somewhere in the same area we were moving, or that I spent last summer there. It just wasn't what I was used to. Indiana had been my home for most of my life. It was what I knew, and Tennessee wasn't going to change that. Not in anyway, shape, or form.

One way or another, I was going to get back to Indiana. I could live with my Uncle Rex if I had to, or my Uncle Wayne and Aunt Tootie. I bet Dad never had to go through this kind of thing when he was growing up. If he had, he would have never done this to us.

It goes without saying all that was how I felt, until I met Jenn.

# CHAPTER TWO

JENNIFER LA'NETTE TATE WAS the most beautiful girl my eyes had ever seen. Blonde, blue eyes, and built like a brick. . .well, you get the picture. She had this sort of a slight accent that held me in its listening power. Every time she spoke. Soft and sweet, like a gentle rain.

The day I met her, I was riding my dirt bike on one of the swimming beaches of the Tennessee River. I just happen to catch sight of her sitting in a lounge chair, in the yard of one of the many summerhouses that dominated the area. I was riding wheelies, making small hill jumps, and just being myself. She on the other hand, was watching me.

She was wearing a white bikini, and pretending to be reading one of those thick romance novels. I say pretending, because she held the book upside down, when she was reading it. I'm really not that good with girls, so it took me several minutes to work up some kind of nerve to introduce myself. Usually with me, when it comes to girls, it takes off right from the start, or it doesn't.

I wasn't sure about this one.

"Hi," I said, pulling my bike into her drive.

"Hi, yourself," she replied, looking over the rim of her shades.

"I saw you from the beach," I said, turning off my bike. "And thought I would come up and introduce myself."

"So, who are you?"

"Ryc Lewis," I said, starting to think that maybe she was someone I didn't really want to know after all.

"Hi, Ryc Lewis," she said, with a smile. "I'm Jennifer Tate. My friends call me Jenn."

"So do I call you Jenn, or Jennifer?"

"That depends," she smiled again, and I'm sure I must have started turning a shade of red. "Are you gonna be my friend, or something else?"

"I'll be your friend," I replied, shyly. "I'm not to up on the or something else gig."

"You're not from around here, are ya?" she asked.

"I could say the same thing about you," I said. "Folks from the South don't sound the way you do."

"Nor do they sound like a Yankee," she smiled.

"Okay," I said. "The answer to your question is, yes and no. I was born here, but I grew up in Indiana."

"That's about like me," she laughed. "I was born here too. Only I grew up in the grand old country called Canada."

"Then I guess we have something in common," I said, swinging my leg over the bike, so I could lean against it. "I'm a transplanted Yankee, and you're a whole lot more transplanted Yankee than I am. Seeing how Canada is way up North and all."

"I guess we do have something in common," she laughed. "So, how long have you been here?"

"About two weeks, I think," I replied. "I was here last summer staying with my uncle, as kind of a get use to it deal that I wasn't told about. That's because at the time, I never dreamed I'd end up living here."

"Do you like it?"

"It's okay," I stated, to be honest. "It's just not what I'm used to."

"I love it," she confessed. "We just got here a couple of days ago. It's the first time we've been here in years."

"Why so long?"

5

"My mother died here, three years ago," she said, looking out toward the river. "Neither my father, nor I could get up the nerve to come back."

"So what changed your minds?"

"Dad's thinking about selling the place," she said.

"Do you want him to sell it?" I asked, hoping that she would rather he not.

"I don't really know," she replied. "A part of me wants to hold onto the memories, and another part of wants to forget. Sometimes it hurts to remember."

"Guess you're just getting here's why I haven't seen you around," I said, and straddled my bike. I figured if she weren't going to be around that long, it wouldn't be a good idea to get too attached.

My Dad would be overjoyed, and I really didn't need a broken heart.

"But. . ." she smiled, as if she had read my thoughts. "We might decide to stay."

"Really," I said, swinging my leg back over the bike.

"Yeah," she said. "My Dad's job just got transferred to Nashville. So, there's a chance that we might decide to stay."

After that, being in Tennessee really wasn't as bad as I thought it was going to be. Especially, seeing how a nobody punk like me could make such good friends with a beautiful girl like Jennifer Tate. I mean, seriously, she and I would have never even spoke if we were in Indiana. That's just the way it was there.

So why did I really want to stay in Indiana? I really wasn't sure.

I didn't hold myself too highly, because no one ever really paid me that much mind back in Indiana. Especially the girls. I'm not sure, but I think it had a lot to do with the way I looked, and dressed. Long hair like an Indian's, ragged blue jeans, a white T-shirt, my black leather jacket (not so much in the Tennessee summer heat) and black motorcycle boots. You know, the classic James Dean and Elvis look.

I guess I was either too poor, or too much like a hood to have the girls associate with me on a boyfriend level. Like all things about me, it was just an image that I maintained. I walked quietly, spoke softly, and played a loud guitar. It was kind of how I kept the other bad asses off my back when I didn't want to play their games.

My Uncle Rex said that it produced a certain amount of unknown fear that kept people wondering what I was all about. He said it was a

Lewis family trait among the men that caused people to wonder, or worry about what we were going to do next. Personally, I think it's an age-old reputation that just hangs on like a bad dream. A dream we all end up having to live up to, or face up to eventually.

In reality, I'm actually a humble hearted soul that doesn't really like to have all that much attention. Except for when I'm playing my music. I write my songs, ride my bike, and stay pretty much to myself. That's mostly because the rest of the world doesn't see things the way I do. That's why folks say I'm strange.

That's because they don't know me. They never took the time.

No one has ever taken the time to really know the real me, and I've never really given them a chance. Not even with the few friends I allowed myself to have. I guess that's partly why my friends back in Indiana meant so much to me. I was afraid I wouldn't get the chance to know anyone else the way I knew them.

Guess I was wrong about that one.

## CHAPTER THREE

I GUESS YOU COULD say we started going together after that first meeting, because we spent the next three days together, from early in the morning until late afternoon. It seemed like we never ran out of things to talk about, or share with each other. You might think I'm over reacting when I say this, but it was honestly like we were meant to find each other on the shores of that river. It was like our two lives had come into existence just for that purpose.

I was truly in a world I had never really been in before with a girl. I wouldn't do it any true justice, to try to repeat everything we said to each other. It was obvious we were falling in love, and that was all that really mattered. I knew what train I was on, and knew that I wasn't going to get off of it by my own free will. That was the magic of what I felt for her, and by the way she came across to me, I believed she felt the same way.

"What's your most favorite thing about being alive?" She asked, one afternoon, as we sat on this weird rock formation we all called "The Thinking Rock."

"You," I replied, as she slipped her hand into mine, and my fingers wrapped around it like a glove.

"No, Silly," she said, looking around at the beauty of the sight that surrounded us. "What would you like to do, if you were alone, and could do your most favorite thing in the world?"

"That's a hard one," I said, and gave it some thought. "I guess if it isn't playing my guitar, I'd like to go walking in the rain."

"I love to walk in the rain," she said, with a sparkle in her eye. "It gives me a strange peace of mind that I can't find any other time."

"I think it makes me think better," I said. "You know, with a clear picture of what's going on around me."

"Yeah," she smiled, from ear to ear. "That's exactly what I mean by having a strange peace of mind."

Her father was gone a lot on business in Nashville; so I really hadn't been introduced to him, accept in passing. Meaning, I would walk into the yard, and he would drive passed me on his way out. He seemed to be a nice enough person, who always had a warm smile. It did, however, make me wonder about him a little, because here I was this long-haired hippy type, left alone time and time again, with his only daughter.

It just didn't seem right to me. Then again, I tend to question everything, and look for answers, or reasons that aren't there. Aside from being in my head.

I knew, however, that sooner or later, we were going to come face to face in conversation, and it scared the hell out of me. I mean the thought of it really spooked me. I had no idea what I would say, or how I would act. I had never had to meet a girl's parents before, and somehow knew it was gonna be one of those virgin moments where I would think, "Oh, my God, this is it."

"My Dad wants to meet you," Jenn said. "He's gonna be here all weekend, and is expecting you to come over for lunch on Saturday."

"Is he cool?" I asked. "I mean, he's not one of those crazy types that gives you the third degree or anything, is he?"

"No," she laughed. "My Dad's real cool. I think you're going to like each other just fine. That is if he doesn't start thinking about the last guy who liked me."

"What do you mean?" I asked.

"Daddy didn't like the idea that he liked touching me," she smiled.

"Great," I said. "What broke the camel's back, and ended your relationship?"

"I'm not really sure," she said, and suddenly broke into laughter. "They're still looking for his body."

"Good one," I said, shaking my head. "You had me dancin' on air."

"My Dad's a sweet heart," Jenn said. "You'll get along just fine."

"I hope so," I said, with a sigh. "Because to tell you the truth, I'm real chicken about this."

"Don't be," she said, and laid her head on my chest. "If I love you, so will he."

If I love you, she said. Did she, or didn't she? That was the question. It was also the first time I had let the thought really cross my mind. Okay, okay, I know. It was more than likely just my nerves getting the best of me. I have a right to feel confused and all tied up inside, don't I? I mean, I am in love, you know.

If she didn't love me, then we would never be acting the way we were toward each other. We'd more than likely be at each other's throats. Yet, there were other things that suddenly made me start to wonder about it all. Things like, she never talked about being in love with me, until just then. Also, we had yet to take our first kiss.

Oh, man, I've never kissed a girl before. Not a real flesh and blood girl. I've only kissed pictures of Julie Andrews and Lynn Anderson. Oh, yeah, I did have a pretty mean crush on Susan Dey, and Batgirl. What guy doesn't? Only kissing posters wasn't the same as kissing the real thing.

Maybe she was waiting on me to make the first move? Maybe she was wondering the same thing about me? Oh, boy, oh, boy, I ain't ever made that kind of move before. What if I did something wrong? What if she didn't like the way I kissed? What if she. . . man, I needed to think about all this.

I mean I seriously needed to think about it.

I can see it all clearly now. We're alone in her room, or out on the deck, when the big moment takes place. I land my lips on her, like I was kissing one of my posters, and she pulls away from me with such a start, that we both fell, crashing to the floor. She's laughing her head off, and I was crying up a storm.

"You call that a kiss?" she said, still laughing.

"I've never kissed a real girl before," I would say, trying to defend myself.

"What?" she would laugh even harder. "I think maybe you had better go back home to your posters, and let me find a real man."

"No!" I screamed, and snapped out of it.

Okay, so I was pushing it with my imagination. Love makes you do crazy things, or at least that's what the general idea is. I needed to talk to someone. Someone I could trust, who would understand where I was coming from. The only person I could think of was Debbi, but she was nearly fourteen miles away, and I wasn't likely to see her anytime soon.

The only other person was Carol Anne. The only problem with that was, she wasn't back from her family vacation yet. I know that because, I went over to her house the second day I was in Tennessee, and was told by her neighbor. So there I was stuck again without a paddle, or any clue what so ever as to what I was going to do.

When all else fails, you wing it. I wonder how fast I can grow me a pair of wings. Can I order them, or do they just appear?

Man, I hope mine don't turn out to be chicken wings.

# CHAPTER FOUR

JUST A FEW DAYS before the big meeting with her father, she went with him to Nashville for a couple days. It was one of the most trying times of my life. I honestly didn't know what to do with myself. Between dealing with my two little brothers and missing her, I was gonna end up going insane. Love and little brothers can do that to a guy, you know.

Anyway, I found myself sitting on the front porch, with my guitar a lot the days she was gone. It seemed to be the only way I could escape the rest of the world. Besides, it wasn't raining, and I didn't really have any other choice for myself.

I was working on one of my songs, just before dinner, when I heard this voice from the past call out my name. It was Carol Anne Oddley, my best friend from the summer before, when I stayed down here with Uncle Pete. If anyone in the world knew me at all, I would lay odds that she was probably the only one that had any kind of handle on it.

"Carol Anne?" I called back to her, filled with a new magic. "It's about time you got back from wherever it was you were."

"Blame my Dad," she said.

She'd been spending the first part of summer on vacation with one of her aunt's in Memphis, when I first got there. At that moment, I missed seeing her, almost as much as I missed Jenn. In fact, much to my regret, since my relationship with Jenn, I hadn't really thought about her that much. A sad piece of reality that I would never tell her, because of what she meant to me as a friend. I was the only one who knew, and the only one who had to know.

"I'd been back two weeks ago," she said, coming up on the porch to sit next to me. "If my Dad hadn't decided to stay on, and help my aunt out a little longer than expected."

"Well, you're here now," I said, and gave her a welcoming hug. "Man, I've missed you."

"I'm so glad your family moved down here," she said. "I was getting to the point where I hated the thought of writing letters to you, because it made me miss you that much more."

"I know what you mean," I confessed. "To be perfectly honest with you, you were the only thing I missed about Tennessee."

"Gee," she laughed. "With you being such a big Elvis fan and all, I would tend to think you'd miss that more."

"I didn't want to tell you that part," I smiled, and she quickly punched me in the arm.

"Thanks a lot," she added, to the punch.

"Hey," I said, grabbing my arm. "That' my strummin' arm, you know."

"What was that you were playin' when I walked up?" she asked, changing the subject a little. "It sounded good."

"One of my songs," I replied.

"One of your songs?" she questioned. "Are you tellin' me you actually started writing your own songs?"

"Finally," I smiled. "Would you like to hear it?"

"Would I?" she asked, as if she couldn't believe I had asked her such an easy question. "You know I loved hearing you play, when you were playing other people's songs. To hear one of your original tunes would be an honor."

"Don't laugh," I warned her. "I'm still working on it, and ain't quite sure of my own style just yet."

"I'd never laugh at one of your songs," she said, leaning back against the corner post to listen.

> "I've seen the rain fallin' down
> I've listened with my heart
> And I've been lost in the lost and found
> With my eyes wide open in the dark
> Until I heard a stranger say
> While callin' out my name
> That the night and day
> Had always been the same
> It just depends on the way
> You let yourself see
> If you ever really want to pay
> Attention to what you see
> For all it's worth
> And all its avenues
> This mother Earth
> Has a lot to choose
> Cause it looks the same on me
> As it's gonna look on you
> Yeah, it looks the same on me
> As it's gonna look on you."

"That's all I've got right now," I said, strumming to a finish. "I expect to write maybe one or two more verses, before I'm completely done with it."

"It sounds good to me," she said. "Only it's not really the kind of song I picture you writing."

"Okay," I smiled. "What kind of song do you picture me writing?"

"Love songs," she replied. "When you were playin' other people's songs, you played love songs."

"Leave it to you to remember that," I said.

"Have you written any love songs, Ryc?" she asked, all starry eyed and off somewhere I didn't know.

"As a matter of fact," I said. "I've written several love songs."

"Would you play me one?" she asked.

"Sure," I said, and started strumming a song I'd written for Jenn.

"What do you see?
When you look into my eyes
Could it be?
Something you fantasize
I wanna know, I wanna know
What words do you hear?
When I say, "I love you"
Is that a happy tear?
I see fallen from you
I wanna know, I wanna know
What do you feel?
When you're touching me
Is this love for real?
Meant always to be
I wanna know, I wanna know
I wanna know, I wanna know
C'mon, Baby, tell me so
I wanna know, I wanna know
C'mon, Baby, let me know."

"I like the beginning of it," she smiled. "The end kind of cranks a little too much for the rest of the song, if you know what I mean."

"Yeah, I know," I said. "I'm just trying to express the need to know."

"Don't get me wrong," she said. "I really like the song. In fact, I love it."

"Everything I do sounds good to you," I said, with a laugh.

"Who inspired it?" she asked.

"What do you mean?"

"I get the feeling that when you write a song," she said. "It's either about someone, or something. That's a someone song."

"How do you figure?" I asked, wondering how she could know something like that, and have only heard two of my songs.

"It's the same with the other song," she said. "Whoever this person is, they've touched you in such away, that you've opened your eyes to see things you haven't seen before, and now are hungering to know more."

15

"I met this girl down on the river," I confessed. "I guess we're kind of going together now. It's one of those relationships that just happens out of the blue."

"Who is she?" Carol Anne asked, excitedly. "Maybe I know her."

I don't know what I was thinking, because for some unknown reason, I was almost afraid to let her know I had a girlfriend. It was like I was betraying her, or something stupid like that. Only I know I wasn't. Carol Anne and I have never been on the level of lovers. We had this best friend gig going, and that's how I pictured us. So why this crazy feeling all of the sudden? Maybe I was just afraid it would change our friendship, or something to that effect. Things change things all around us every day, without our ever-knowing why.

I guess what I'm trying to say is, I loved Carol Anne as if she were a part of me, and I didn't want to lose that. Like with my friends back in Indiana, I didn't want to lose what we already shared. Besides, I'd already given up more than I wanted to.

"Jennifer Tate," I replied.

"Jenn's back?" she asked, jumping up from where she sat. "I can't believe this. It's been like forever since I saw her last."

"I guess that means you know her," I said, with a smile.

At least what I had feared in the beginning wasn't the way it was going. Besides that, it really didn't surprise me all that much that Carol Anne knew her. She was the kind of person who knew everybody. Even the people she's never met. It was one of those things that went against her quiet personality, and yet, expressed it so well.

"Let's go pay her a visit," Carol Anne said, taking a step off the porch.

"We can't," I said. "She went with her Dad to Nashville on business, and won't be back until Friday afternoon."

"Man," she said, really disappointed like, and sat back down.

"Sorry," I said.

"I can't believe she's back," she said, almost talking to herself. "What's it been? Two, maybe three years?"

"Three years," I said, reminding her that I was there. "She told me about her mother dying, and how they didn't come back because of it."

"Yeah," Carol Anne replied. "That was a really sad time, for both her and her Dad."

"I bet it was," I said. "They might be staying this time, because her Dad's job got transferred to Nashville."

"Great," Carol Anne said. "Now I have both my best friends living near me."

"At the same time," I added.

"Imagine that," she smiled. "And they're boyfriend and girlfriend. Who'd ever believe something like that could happen?"

"It blows me away," I said, with a smile of my own.

"I bet it does," Carol Anne said, and looked at me with a look I couldn't quite read.

"What's her father do?" I asked to change the subject. "Jenn's never really said, and I've never really asked."

"He's a record producer and talent scout," she replied. "He's just the kind of man you need to know. He could probably help make your music into a real career."

"I guess so," I said, thinking about it. "I don't want that to become the reason I'm involved with Jenn. I'd rather find my own way to success."

"I kind of figured that," Carol Anne said. "With you being the self-made kind and all, who would rather take the hard way, then get a little help."

See what I mean? Carol Anne knew me better than anyone. Even better than I knew myself at times. That's saying a lot, because a person should really know themselves, if they ever want to get anywhere in life.

"Who's your friend?" Dad asked, standing at the front door.

"Oh, Hi, Dad," I said, a little surprised. "This is Carol Anne, the girl I met here last summer."

He must have over heard us talking, or me playing the guitar. The question was, just how much had he listened to, before making his presence known? I was worried that he might have heard about Jenn, and that if he did, there would be hell to pay. My Dad was a real bastard, when it came to keeping an eye on me, and the girl's I hung out with. Which were really not that many, because I knew how he was, and knew it wouldn't go over too well.

"Hi, Carol Anne," Dad said.

"Nice to meet you, Mr. Lewis," Carol Anne replied.

"Like wise," he said, and then looked at me. "Your Mom will have dinner ready in a few minutes."

"Okay," I said, as he went back into the darkness of the living room.

He had a language that you had to read between the lines, if you wanted to understand what he was actually saying. In other words, Mom probably just started dinner. What he was saying was, he wanted me to send Carol Anne on her way.

"He looks mean," Carol Anne said, in almost a whisper.

"He can be," I stated, in almost the same whisper. "But he's okay, most of the time."

"When is he not?" she asked.

"When I'm with a girl," I replied.

"He sounds like my Dad," she said. "Only it's when I'm with a boy."

"It's gonna make hell on our relationship," I said. "Do you think we'll ever survive it?"

"Yeah," she said. "We just have to be sneaker than they are."

"Right," I laughed.

"Look," she said. "Mom's probably got our dinner finished too."

"Does that mean you're leaving?"

"I was supposed to be gone only a few minutes," she said, getting up to go. "We'll have to get together sometime, okay? Sometime when our parents aren't in control of the moment."

"I'm sure we will," I said.

I noticed something in her voice that I didn't like. Like maybe she thought our friendship wouldn't be the same as it was last year, now that Jenn and I were together, and our parents were going to be around. I didn't like it, because I didn't want our relationship to turn out that way. Carol Anne was an important part of my life. I needed her to always be a part of it.

"How about tomorrow," I called.

"What time?" she called back.

"Surprise me," I said, and watched her wave good-bye, as she topped the hill that kept us from seeing each other's houses.

I didn't know where the path a head of me was going to lead. I just knew that I was on it, and was going to follow it wherever it led. I did know that I was treading dangerous waters, with my Dad, and the two relationships I was having with girls. The thing is, I'd been drilled so much by my Dad's doing the right thing, and keeping my thing in my pants, that I believed I could just about handle anything. The question was, how sure was I? I mean, I knew that I didn't want to take any chances that could wash away my dreams, but it didn't mean I didn't want to have a girlfriend either. We may be young, and full of cum like our parent's tend to say. My Dad for one, if you really must know. But at the same time, I believe we know the limits. It's a different generation. It's not the same as it was in his day, or their day. Hopefully, we've learned from their mistakes. At least, I think I have.

At least I hope so.

# CHAPTER FIVE

I WENT INTO DINNER thinking things were gonna be okay. Carol Anne was back, we were still best friends, and she liked my girlfriend. That was the way life was meant to be. Sweet, without conflict, and straight ahead.

I'd forgotten about my Dad.

Unfortunately, the above wouldn't be how the rest of the evening went. My Dad was in one of those mean moments, and I was gonna be the butt end of his attack. Lately, that seems to be the way it went, when he got to thinking about girls and me. Especially, now that I was well into the start of my teen-age years.

"I'm only gonna tell you this once," he said, as I sat down at the kitchen table. "That Carol Anne is a really nice lookin' girl. So if you two go to messin' around. It's your baby, not mine. You'll have to deal with it on your own."

"She's just a friend, Dad," I said, a little disturbed by what he was saying. "We don't think of each other in that way."

"Friendships tend to change," he said. "One day you're acting like brother and sister, then the next day you're in the back seat of your buddy's car doing the wild thing."

"What's the wild thing?" I asked, trying to be as stupid as he sounded.

"Don't get smart with me, Mister," he snapped. "Or I'll see to it that you never leave this house again."

"C'mon, Dad," I pleaded. "Give me a break. I've got more marbles in my head than that. I want to do something with my life."

"You're right," he said. "You do have more marbles than that. It's just that, that thing in your pants has a mind of it's own. When it starts talking, you lose control of those other marbles you're so keen to point out."

"Dad?" I pleaded, even harder. "It's not like that with us."

"Yeah," he smiled. "How do you think you got here?"

"Thanks," I said, standing up from the table. "That's a really great thing to tell one of your kids. Especially, when you're bitching at him about sex."

"The truth is the truth," he said, staring at me. "It's something you would have figured out sooner or later. You weren't a plan child, Ryc. You were a wild night out in the back seat of one of your uncle's cars."

"I've had enough of this," I said, so close to tears I couldn't bare it, and headed for my room. "I hope that makes you real proud of yourself."

"Aren't you going to eat your supper?" Mom asked, with a worried look on her face.

She worried way too much, and I hated making her worry about anything. It's just that we both knew not to cross the line with him too far. Mom knew even better than I did, what kind of ass hole he could become, if confronted with his issues, and that was something he was always right about. I've been hit too many times, not to know what I'm talking about. Mr. James Lewis often thought he was God of his little corner of the world, and never let any of us forget it.

"Did you hear your mother?" he yelled.

"I'm suddenly not that hungry," I said, and kept going.

"Good," he said. "You can stay that way until morning. If you can't eat when your mother puts it on the table, then you don't need to eat at all."

"Fine," I said, and slammed my door.

"Why do you do that to him, Jim?" I heard Mom ask.

"You know damn well why I do it," he snapped. "If I don't keep on him about it, he's gonna end up being in more trouble than either of us wants."

"Yes," Mom said, sarcastically. "Especially, since he's the only one that does stay out of trouble."

"Good for you, Mom," I said, while sitting on my bed, against the backboard.

Smack! He hit her, because she stood up for me.

"It's between me and him," he yelled, after hitting her. "Now, stay out of it."

"Mom?" I asked, stepping out of my room.

"She's okay," Dad said.

"He hit her," Joe said, crying.

"If you want to hit someone," I yelled. "Try hitting me. She's already been hit, once too often because of your temper."

"Go to bed, Ryc," he said, in a lower tone.

"Mom?" I asked again.

"I'm okay," she said, with a sob.

"Are you sure?"

"Go to bed," said Dad, in a more irritated tone.

"Okay," I said, and went back into my room.

He really pissed me off, when he did stuff like that. I was getting to the age where I wasn't going to allow much more of it. Sooner or later, he and I were gonna butt heads really hard, and I'm sure they both knew it as well as I did.

In my room, I sat back down on the bed, and started playing my guitar. That's what I did, when I was upset about something. I played my guitar really hard, and fast. No one could touch me when I was in that world. It was a lot like walking in the rain.

"If you can't eat," Dad called out, so I was sure to hear him. "You can't play that damn guitar either."

"Go to hell," I said, under my breath, and kept playing.

"I told you, you couldn't play that thing," he yelled, after busting through the door. "Now put the thing up, or lose it period."

"Why are you doing this?" I asked, with hatred in my eyes.

"You don't get to ask questions," he said, and took the guitar anyway.

See what I mean? He can be real mean at times. He starts something, and then makes everyone else pay for it. It was like he didn't have a heart at times, and could careless how the rest of us felt about it. Our feelings weren't anything that mattered, when he got that way. We were only stepping stones, for him to walk on.

I know he thinks I'm stupid. That I'm gonna be like he was, when it came to dealing with girls, and ruin my life too. Why? I kept asking myself. I'm not like him. I'm not living his life, and he's not gonna live mine.

I have more important things to do with my life than to waste it on things I'm not ready for. Being in love, or even being with a girl doesn't mean I have to be having sex with her.

Does it?

There's more to being in love, then getting laid. Sure, I think about those kind of things, but that's not what I'm about. I'm about being alive, and sharing my life with the folks I love. Showing them that there's more to me, then what I'm given credit for.

Why can't he see that?

His repeated attacks on me about sex have almost turned me completely away from it, or maybe it's the other way around? Maybe I should be thinking more about it? Maybe I should start thinking about it the way he thinks I do?

Maybe he would be happy then?

Maybe one of these days, he'll grow up, and see me for the man I am? Instead of the one he thinks he sees in me. Maybe he'll understand who I am?

Until then, I guess I'll just have to put up with him, and stay in the battle I did not start. I'd rather walk away from it, instead of being one of its pawns. One of his pawns, in a war that he makes harder on everyone. Including him. I hope I'm strong enough to wait for him, to at least try to see it my way.

That is, if he ever grows up.

"Ryc?" Mom asked, from the other side of the door.

"Come in," I called.

"Are you, okay?" she asked, walking in with my guitar.

"I'm okay," I replied. "The question is, how are you?"

"I'm used to the way he is," she said, handing me my guitar. "Here, put this up for a while."

"How'd you get it back from him?" I asked, laying it on the bed.

"I told him he didn't need to take your guitar," she said. "Just because he was upset by the fact you were growing up."

"Thanks," I said.

"Just take it easy when you're out with that girl."

"She's my friend, Mom," I said, as a few tears ran down my cheek.

"What are you crying for?" she asked, and wiped the tears away with her fingers.

"I hate it when he hits you," I said.

"I know," she said, and hugged me close to her. "Maybe one of these days he'll out grow it, and see things the way they really are."

"I hope so," I said, and held onto her for a very long moment.

Mom was a stronger woman, than any one of us was aware of. She had to be, to put up with my Dad for all the years that she had been with him. I know, that deep down inside, she was getting really tired of it. I can't say it's true, but if any of the rumors I've heard about her going to the arms of another man were true, I couldn't blame her. I know it's wrong, but then so is the way my Dad continues to act.

I love them both very much. It's just that sometimes, there comes a moment when we should turn our backs on some things. It doesn't go without saying, that I've heard the same rumors about him cheating on her.

Rumors have away of doing something to a person's heart. I don't know how they were gonna affect me, but I had this strange unsettling feeling that in the long run, they were going to change the way I viewed things. Even though I understood the reasons why the rumors were there, they forged themselves into my thoughts, and I knew that I would never be the one who would just up and cheat on the person I loved.

Especially, someone I was married to.

# CHAPTER SIX

CAROL ANNE CAME PECKING on my window, at a quarter 'til eight. I was so tired from staying up half the night that I tried to ignore her. Which was something you don't do with Carol Anne Oddley, once she got into your life.

When she didn't get me to respond, she climbed through the window, and into bed with me. I didn't really think about it, because it was something she had done several times, the summer before. Remember, what kind of relationship we shared. It was one that seems to make us one in the same, and a part of each other.

Laying, or sleeping in the same bed was no big deal to us. My father on the other hand, would have blown his stack. Especially, after what we had gone through the night before. I guess in some unknown since, I may have had a death wish going for me.

But then again, I wasn't thinking about it.

"Are you going to wake up, Sleep Head?" she asked, whispering in my ear.

"Give me a minute," I said back to her, not quite registering where she was.

"No," she replied, and stuck her wet tongue into my ear.

"Hey," I shouted, and set up in the bed. "Carol Anne? What are you doing here?"

"It's morning," she said. "I'm here to spend the day with you."

"I'm not dressed," I said, realizing I was still in my underwear.

"So," she smiled. "I've seen you naked."

She was right. When I was down here the year before, she and I would sneak out at night, and go skinny-dipping in the Tennessee River. We even played spin the bottle, with my cousin Debbi, and her little sister Vicky. It was just some of the crazy things you do, when you're daring teen-agers. It was the kind of stuff we did, to pass the time away, and never thought twice about it. I mean, what the hell, it was no big deal, and no one was getting hurt.

It wasn't about sex either.

"You're gonna get me killed, "I whispered. "Especially, if my father finds you in here."

"Why are you whispering?"

"I don't want him to catch you in here," I said.

"They're not here," she laughed.

"How do you know they're not here?" I asked, still whispering.

"I watched them and your two brothers leave about twenty minutes ago," she replied. "I would have never come over like this, if they were still here."

"That's nice to know," I said, and flashed her a smile.

"Besides," she frowned. "The entire neighborhood heard your fight with him last night."

"That's good," I said. "Now I have to feel like an idiot, when I run into one of them."

"Everyone's starting to understand the way he is," she reassured me. "It was kind of nice having someone fight over me."

"That's good," I said, climbing out of bed, and slipping my jeans on. "Because I'm really too young to die, if you know what I mean?"

"You still have a nice looking butt," she said. "What I can see of it, anyway."

"Should you be looking at my butt?" I asked, feeling a little bit embarrassed. "I mean, I have a girlfriend, and the last time you wrote me, you had a boyfriend in Memphis."

"I won't tell, if you don't tell," she smiled, innocently. "Besides, we're not having sex, or cheating on them, are we?"

"Not according to my Dad," I said, pulling a T-shirt over my head. "He seems to think we're going to be doing it, sooner or later."

"C'mon," she laughed. "Doesn't he know we're just really good friends?"

"He doesn't look at it that way," I said. "He bases everything on the way he was, when he was a teen-ager."

"Is he stupid?"

"Sometimes, I think he is," I confessed. "As you already know, we kind of had it out last night, because of our relationship."

"Okay, then," she said, and started unbuttoning her blouse. "Maybe we should just have sex, and get it over with."

"Carol Anne?" I asked, with some surprise.

"I'm just joking," she laughed, with her blouse all the way unbuttoned. "You should have seen the look on your face."

"You should have felt the sudden rush I felt," I replied, and hit her with one of my pillows, as she still sat on my bed.

"Hey," she screamed, with yet some more laughter, and jumped out of the bed. "You're not playing fair."

"Oh, yeah," I said, pushing her back down on the bed, so I could pin her down.

Her blouse came all the way open, and showed me that her tits had gotten quite a bit bigger than the last time I saw them. We just kind of froze, as I lay on top her, staring into her eyes, and wondering what was going on.

We stared at each other, for what seemed like an eternity, when my Dad's attacking voice came dancing through my thoughts. "It's your baby, not mine." I heard him say, in the back of my head. It was the first time I came to realize his side of it, or at least what he was talking about. It was one of those moments I wasn't ready for.

Carol Anne still looked like a very young and beautiful June Carter, and I felt something I never thought I would feel. In another place and time, it wouldn't have been all that hard for me to fall in love with her. The only problem with it now was, we were such good friends, and I was already involved with Jenn.

The idea of being something beyond our friendship, made me think that in the end I might lose her, and what we had now. I didn't want to take a chance on losing that part of us.

Therefore, I never allowed myself to think in those kind of terms when it came to us, or when it came to her. Our relationship was beyond the measure of simple words, and that's the way I wanted to keep it. Her friendship meant that much to me, and I was scared as hell that we were this close to crossing over.

"Maybe we should button this up," I said, and started buttoning her blouse, as I sat across her mid section.

"Yeah," she whispered, still staring into my eyes.

"Why are you whispering?" I asked, whispering myself.

"Cause you're sitting on me," she said, and crashed a pillow into the side of my head.

We both started laughing really hard, as I rolled off of her, and onto my back. I was so relieved that we hadn't let ourselves go anywhere else with what had just taken place. I would have never forgiven myself, if it had. She was my friend, and I loved her in more ways than Carter had liver pills.

"I love you, Richart Drake Lewis," she said, rolling up on her side to look me in the face. "You're my best friend, and I don't ever want that to change."

"Me either," I said, and kissed her on the cheek. "C'mon, let's go get a soda, down at the Floating Store."

"After all that laughter, I could use a cold drink."

We both crawled out my bedroom window, and into the only world truly worth sharing with anyone. Our friendship. Sure, it would be tested, time and time again, but it would always come back to what it was. The days ahead, would prove it.

Life was never easy. You would be a fool to consider that it was. We all make our share of mistakes, and choices we have to live with. We all get a little bit weird sometimes, and we all take for granted what we think is so. I know, I've been down that path many times, and it still amazes me that I can still wind up there.

What took place in my bedroom was a test. A test that two very dear friends challenged, and won in spite of how tempting it might have been. Regardless of what you might think, we both knew what it could have cost us in the end.

A price neither one of us wanted to pay, or was even ready for.

# CHAPTER SEVEN

"SO WHAT ARE YOU going to do, if she wants to kiss you?" Carol Anne asked, as we headed toward the Floating Store.

"Kiss her, I guess," I replied, not sure what brought this on.

"And how many girls have you ever kissed?" she asked, not really looking at me.

"None," I confessed. I knew this didn't mean kissing my Mom, or one of my aunts on the cheek.

"Here," she said, stopping in the middle of the road, and got up real close to me. "Put your arms around my waist."

"Like this?" I asked, as I put my arms around her, and she put hers around my neck.

"Now kiss me the way you think you would kiss her," she said, staring into my eyes.

"I can't do that," I said, and pulled away from her.

"Look," she said. "I know you like Jenn. That's why I'm trying to make sure you do it right. You don't want to make any stupid mistakes do you?"

"I'll do all right," I said.

"Okay," she said. "But don't forget, you're the one who said you've never kissed a girl before."

She made a very good point that I was starting to see I couldn't get around.

"Okay," I said, and went back up to her. "Show me what I need to know."

"It ain't gonna hurt you," she smiled, as we got back into having our arms around each other. "Now kiss me the way you think you would kiss her."

This time, we were both staring at each other. We were closer than we had ever been before. Even closer than we were when we were on my bed earlier. I was starting to feel hot inside, as I pressed my lips to hers. The kiss lasted maybe twenty seconds, before she pulled away from me, and started laughing.

"What's wrong?" I asked.

"You actually call that a kiss?" she answered, with a question of her own. "That's how you would kiss your Mom, or an aunt that you really didn't want to kiss in the first place."

"Okay," I said, feeling a little hurt. "I guess you're going to have to teach me. Since you're the one, who started this."

"Since you're my best friend and all," She smiled. "I guess I can do that."

"Don't laugh at me again," I said.

"Just do what I do," she said, moving back into that arm gig we were in.

This kiss was open mouth, with a hungrier feel to it. Packed with an emotion and power I had never known before. It lasted a lot longer than the first kiss, and caused me to start hearing music in the back of my head.

She pushed away from me, and stepped back like there was something wrong. Her eyes were closed, and she was breathing really hard. When she realized I was watching her, she turned away from me, and didn't say a word.

"Did I do something wrong?" I asked.

"No," she said. "You just learn really fast."

"Cool," I said, stepping around her, so I could see her face.

She had a stream of tears running down her face.

"What just happened?" I asked.

"We kissed," she said, and wiped her eyes.

"Are you all right?" I asked, starting to feel a little concerned. Confused was more like it.

"It's nothing," she said, and took off toward her house.

"Carol Anne?" I called after her, but she kept going. "What about the soda?"

Oh, my God, I suddenly realized. Like a slap in the face, I knew what the problem was. How could I have been so blind? There was more to the way Carol Anne felt for me, than I allowed myself to see. She was in love with me.

If I had known, I would have never let her kiss me. Especially, not the way we just did. I really couldn't imagine how she felt, and that made me hurt for her.

She was my best friend. Stepping over the line into a relationship with her would change everything. I wouldn't ever be able to think of her the same way, if I let that happen. We wouldn't be the same people.

I didn't want to hurt her either. I could never purposely hurt her. I loved her too much, as a friend. I suddenly realized that I didn't know what to do, or make of all of this. To say it left me in a state of confusion would be an understatement. I was more than just confused. I was totally and uncontrollably lost.

Besides, I loved Jenn.

So what was the deal with the music playing in my head? Was there more to the way I felt about Carol Anne that I wasn't allowing myself to see? No, no, no, I couldn't allow myself to start thinking about things like that. It was. . .

Man, growing up was getting harder and harder to deal with. Why wasn't there a set of rules to follow? At least something that would make things move a little easier than this.

There was. Don't go around kissing your best friend.

"Hey, Ryc?" called my cousin, Debbi Roberson. Uncle Pete's oldest daughter.

"Hey," I called back to her, hoping that she hadn't seen Carol Anne and I kissing.

She meant well, but something like this was just too much to hold in. Sooner or later, she would let it slip out, and my Dad would get wind of it. If that happens, all hell would break loose, and I would never hear the end of it. In fact, I would probably never see the light of day again.

Believe me. I know this to be true.

"Did I just see what I think I saw?" she asked, walking up with her boyfriend.

She saw us kissing.

"It wasn't what you thought it was," I stated.

"It looked like a passionate kiss to me," she smiled.

"Yeah," said her boyfriend, Donny Long. "It also looked like there was some trouble at brew. By the way she took off."

"There's more to it than that," I said, not really wanting to get into it with them.

"Don't sweat it, Man," Donny said. "We all have our ups and downs. Don't we, Babe?"

Donny was a class jerk, in his own league, and was starting to prove it. I didn't see what Debbi saw in him. But then, it was her life, not mine.

"Yeah," Debbi said, looking at him with a really hard look. "We all get into it once in awhile."

"Right," I said, and started on toward the Floating Store.

"Don't let it stress you out, Man," Donny called. "It's just a woman thing."

"Go to hell," I heard Debbi say to him.

Guess they were having one of their ups and downs. It served Donny right, with the off the wall and rude remarks he made.

As for me, I had some thinking to do. I'd unwillingly gotten myself into a mess I had never been in before. A mess I had no clue in the world as to working out. Someone, or several someone's were going to get hurt, and I wanted no part of it.

The only thing was, I somehow felt like I was the reason for it all, and that alone made it my fault. What was I going to do? What was I thinking, letting myself kiss Carol Anne like that? Why hadn't I notice the way she felt about me? How was I ever going to explain this to Jenn, if she ever found out what happened?

Maybe I should just shoot myself, and get it over with.

# CHAPTER EIGHT

When I came out of the Floating Store with my soda, I saw this guy about my age, working on his dirt bike. He had long brown hair, a little shorter than mine, and seemed to be having some trouble with his bike.

"What's the problem?" I asked, walking up to him.

"The damn thing won't run," he said, looking up at me. "I think the fuel line is clogged."

"No tools, right?" I asked, trying to insert some humor.

"Yeah," he laughed. "And I live about ten miles from here."

"That's a problem," I laughed, and reached into my front pocket for my pocket knife. "Here, maybe this'll help."

"Thanks, Man," he replied, took the knife, and had it fixed within a matter of seconds.

"At least now you won't have to push it home," I said, as he handed my knife back.

"What's your name?" he asked.

"Ryc Lewis," I replied, offering him my hand.

"Roy Miller," he said, as we shook hands. "Do you live around here?"

"Yeah," I said. "Just up the road, in Woodland Shores."

"Get on," he offered. "I can at least give you a ride home."

"Cool," I said, climbing on the back. "I have a bike of my own."

"What the hell you walkin' for?"

"It's a long story," I said, as we took off.

"We've all got a few of them," he yelled, over the roar of his bike.

He rode like I did, with no rules. Just flat out into the wind, with no fears. It was the only way to be, when you rode a bike.

"Here it is," I said, as we got within sight of the house.

"Ain't this where the Roberson girls live?" he asked, pulling to a stop.

"It used to be," I replied. "They're my cousins, and just moved into Parsons."

"Why?" he asked.

"Who knows?" I asked. "Would you like to come in for a while?"

"Sure," he said, parking the bike. "I can't stay too long. My Dad will have the law out looking for me, if I'm not home by dinner time."

"You have one of those too," I said, with a laugh, as we headed through the house to my room.

"A crazy one at that," he stated.

"Who's your friend?" Mom asked, meeting us in the kitchen hallway.

"Mom, this is Roy Miller," I introduced. "Roy, this is my Mom."

"Nice to meet you, Mrs. Lewis," Roy said.

"You too," she smiled.

"We're going into my room for a few minutes," I said, not knowing what else to say.

"That'll be fine," she said, and we continued on our way.

"What kind of music do you listen to?" he asked, once we got into my room.

"Mostly rock and roll," I said. "But I'll listen too just about anything, if it sounds good."

"You sound like me," he smiled, noticing my guitars. "Do you play?"

"I try to," I replied. "I've got no formal training or anything. Just what I can pick up by ear."

"It's easier to use your fingers," he smiled.

"You've got that right," I replied, with a laugh.

"That's pretty much how I learned to play the bass," he said, and picked up my electric guitar.

"I write my own songs," I added. "Figured if I ever really wanted to get anywhere with it that was something I needed to do."

"Jack off, Booga Lou," he sang, strumming a few bars of Ringo Starr's song, "Back Off, Booga Lou."

"That's pretty cool," I laughed. "Maybe we should get together sometime, and see what we can come up with."

"Sure," he replied, setting my guitar back on its stand. "Or maybe we could go riding sometime."

"That works for me," I said.

"Why don't you play me one of your songs?" Roy asked. "I'm kind of interested in if I like your style or not."

"Why not?" I smiled, picked up my electric guitar, and turned it on. "Rock and Roll, or Country?"

"Rock and Roll, Man."

"Rock and Roll it is," I said, and kicked into gear.

"Hey, Baby, have you heard the news
We're finally old enough to choose
What kind of music we want to hear
And how to face the destiny we fear
Momma no longer rocks the cradle
And Daddy can't enforce his kind of truth
We've lived too many years under that label
And now it's time to breakaway from our youth
We're all grown up
With no place to go
Love has filled the cup
And sex is taking control
We're all grown up
With no place to go
I was thinkin' maybe Nashville or Memphis
Just someplace they ain't gonna miss
Where they'll see how well we've done
When we took our love on the run
But it doesn't really matter to me

As long as it's you I can see
Cause Baby, it's just you and me together
For now, for always, and forever
We're all grown up
With no place to go
Love has filled the cup
And sex is taking control
We're all grown up
With no place to go
So tell me what'd ya say
Are you ready to breakaway
C'mon and take me by the hand
Together we'll work out some kind of plan
Just one more step into tomorrow
And we kiss away our sorrow
Holding on to as far as we can see
Across a bridge into our eternity
We're all grown up
With no place to go
Love has filled the cup
And sex is taking control
We're all grown up
With no place to go
We're all grown up
With no place to go
Love has filled the cup
And sex is taking control
We're all grown up
With no place to go."

"Far out, Man," said Roy, with a big grin after I'd finished.
"You really think so?" I asked.
"You've got it, Dude."
"Cool," I smiled.
"So what's this long story you've got going on?" he asked, leaning up against my dresser.

I told him the entire story about what happen with Carol Anne, and that Jenn was my girlfriend. I felt that the two of us were hitting it off pretty good, and I needed someone to lay the story on. Someone that might understand.

"Sounds like a real headache," he said, when I was finished.

"Or worse," I said.

"Any ideas how you're gonna fix the problem?"

"Not a clue," I replied.

"What the hell," he said. "Why don't you just go with both of them?"

"I can see that happening," I laughed.

"What time is it?"

"Going on noon," I replied, looking at my pocket watch.

"I hate to cut this short," he said. "But I've got to be heading for the house."

"I understand," I replied, as we headed for the front door.

"Let's get together in a few days," he said, on the front porch. "I know some really cool trails over by Sugar Tree."

"Works for me," I said, as he climbed on his bike.

"Maybe we can talk about putting a band together or something," he said. "Or at least jam together for a while."

"That sounds cool," I said, as he kicked started his bike.

"Later," he said, and rode away, with a quick wave good-bye.

Roy Miller was an only child, who lived about a mile and a half from Parsons. The closest big city around for miles. It's also where we would be going to school, when it started back up. He hadn't many friends, because no one understood him, or was into the same kind of stuff he was. Which made him sound a lot like me.

Being somewhat alike made it easier for us to become friends. A friendship I looked forward to seeing grow. Especially, seeing how I didn't have any male friends of my own in Tennessee. He was a welcome change to the way my life with the girls was starting to go, and believe me when I say I felt like I needed a break from it all.

The confusion, and unsure feelings were enough to drive you insane. If things continued down the path they were headed, I was sure that wouldn't be too far off.

Something to look forward to, heh?

# CHAPTER NINE

I WAS SITTING ON the front porch, with my guitar, working on a song, and the nerve to go down to Jenn's to meet her father. A few minutes into the session, I saw Carol Anne coming over the hill toward the house. I was also kind of scared of this meeting with her; because I wasn't sure where it was gonna go.

"Hey," she called, walking up to where I was perched.

"Hey," I said back to her.

"I need to talk to you about yesterday," she said, sitting down next to me. "Is your father around?"

"No," I said. "He's in Lexington."

"Good," she smiled. "I don't think we want him over hearing this."

"Probably not," I said. "Are you, okay?"

"Yeah," she said, and looked the other way for a moment. "That kiss we shared kind of caught me off guard, with feelings I didn't know I had for you."

"I understand," I said, because I didn't know what else to say. "It kind of threw me too."

"I love you, Ryc," she said. "But I'm not sure I love you enough to take a chance on destroying the friendship you and I share."

"I love you too," I said, because I really did. "I thought about the idea of you and me getting together, and was afraid of what it might do to us."

"Why?" she asked, with tears dancing in her eyes.

"Because I knew if we were together," I replied. "Jenn would get hurt, and I couldn't do that to her."

"Yeah," she said, and looked away.

"It hurt me," I said, as she turned back to face me, with flowing tears. "Because I knew you were gonna be hurt by all this. If we were to allow ourselves to fall in love with each other, it would change the way we were, and the friendship we knew would come to an end."

"It might be a better relationship," she said.

"Maybe," I said. "It's just that what I share with you, is one of the most important things in my life, and I would give up loving you to keep it."

"That's why I'm here," she said, noticing that I could no longer contain my own flow of tears. "I feel the same way about you."

"Still friends?" I asked, with a smile.

"Forever," she replied.

"Cool," I said, and gave her a big hug. "Would you look at what cry babies we are?"

"Good tears," she said.

"I guess so," I replied.

"So what were you working on?" she asked, to change the subject.

"A new song," I replied. "I've been trying to put this all down in words, to help me deal with it, and make some logic of it all."

"Can I hear what you've written?" she asked.

"I'm about half way through it," I said.

"I'd like to hear it anyway," she smiled.

"Sure," I said, and picked up my guitar, I had sat against the wall, when she came up. "It's titled, "You Hold On.""

"When it comes to a matter of hearts
All your love and faith fall into parts
When your soul gets ripped away
Into the temptations of another day

Where your dreams start lookin' untrue
And you just don't know what to do
You hold on
Yeah, you hold on
Lookin' for a brand-new start
To put the fire back into your heart
Because even though you do
Losin' ain't for you
You hold on
Yeah, you hold on
Like a dream in the night
You learn to fight
For a reason to be
But still cannot see
Beyond what you already know
Holdin' on in your soul
You hold on
Yeah, you hold on."

"Is that it?" she asked, as I strummed to an end.

"So far," I replied. "I just started it a few minutes before you got here."

"It's what we do," she said, getting up to leave. "I thought it was very beautiful."

"Thanks," I said, pleased with myself.

"Play another song for me, Ryc," she smiled.

"Why?" I asked, not really thinking about an answer.

"I'd just like to hear one."

"Okay," I said, stopped to think for a moment, and then started strumming.

"It's all about the music
It's all about fate
But you can't choose it
In your confused state
You think you know the way
Headed out on your own
Without listening to what they say
Only to end up all alone

Cause you're a rebel without a cause
Breakin' all the laws
Trying to be who you wanna be
The same one no one else can see
Who breaks all the laws
Like a rebel without a cause
You know I've done it to
Playing that game of runaway
Oh, I was just like you
I didn't want to play
Lost myself time and time again
Dazed and confused
Wondering where I'd been
And not at all amused
Cause you're a rebel without a cause
Breakin' all the laws
Trying to be who you wanna be
The same one no one else can see
Who breaks all the laws
Like a rebel without a cause."

"How's that?" I asked when I finished the song.

"Where do you get your ideas?" she asked, shaking her head. "The things you're writing seem to be way beyond what you should know at your age."

"I don't get my ideas," I replied. "They just kinda find me, and then I put them down on paper."

"That's crazy," she laughed.

"So am I," I smiled.

"Where are you headed?"

"I figured you were getting ready to go down to Jenn's," she replied.

"Yeah," I said. "To meet her father."

"That'll be interesting," she smiled. "I'll come down later, and surprise her."

"Why don't we go together?" I asked, walking off the porch with her.

"Are you sure you want me to go with you?" Carol Anne asked.

"What do you think?" I asked, pulling her a long.

41

Carol Anne was still my best friend, and I wanted her to know that. As for everything else in my life, I would take it one step at a time, and see where I ended up. Hoping that it would be just as true, as my friendship with her.

Even though we had resolved this issue, I couldn't help but know there would be more questions to come. Why? Because in another place and time, the results might have been different, and I wasn't too sure it was all the way over.

Love is a battlefield. We walk into it blindly, without any true thought as how we walk away from it. Sometimes we look so hard for love to be the way we want it to be that we don't stop long enough for it to become real, or to see just how it really is. We hope for one thing, and never see it become something else. The plain and simple truth to it is, you never really know the answer, until it becomes.

So we learn to live for the moment, and make the best of whatever it is. This one we're walking through right now.

This one, this moment, and the next.

Somewhere a long the way of that path, is an answer waiting to be born. That's provided "you hold on" long enough to let it find you.

# CHAPTER TEN

"So, HOW LONG HAVE you known Ryc?" Jenn asked Carol Anne, as we all sat on the deck of her house. "Since last summer," Carol Anne replied. "He came down from Indiana to stay with his uncle." "I didn't know you knew each other," Jenn smiled. "Seems like it's a very small world we live in."

Something about the way Jenn looked and sounded, whispered that she was thunder struck with a bit of jealousy. I understood why, because Carol Anne is actually a very lovely girl that any guy in his right mind wouldn't mind being with. I found myself not liking her jealousy at all, because it wasn't fair to Carol Anne. She was my friend, my best friend, and I didn't want to see her get hurt.

She had already been hurt enough, because of her feelings for me, and Jenn's jealousy was uncalled for. Especially, seeing how Carol Anne and I, had already been working that issue out. Then again, Jenn was my girlfriend, and I didn't want her to get hurt either.

Unfortunately for me, I knew that wasn't the way it was gonna play. Lately, nothing seemed to want to play the way I wanted it to.

In matters such as this, girls wrote their own rules. They called all the shots, and let you know with every breath how it was going to be. That's the one thing I was learning about having a girlfriend that I didn't like.

"Here comes my Dad," Jenn said, changing the air we were getting into, when his car pulled into the drive.

He had gone out for some soda, and things to grill out for our lunch. So, I still had not actually met him yet. He was a clean-cut man that looked like he was somewhat better off, than most the other men I knew. That in itself, made me feel that much more out of place. If it wasn't for his warm smile, I would have probably felt completely lost.

"Hello," he said, climbing out of the car.

"Look who came down with Ryc," Jenn said, as we all walked down to give him a hand carrying in things.

"Carol Anne, right?" he asked, with a smile.

"Yeah," she said, and shook the hand he offered her.

"You've grown into quite a beautiful young lady since the last time I saw you," he said. "But then, we all grow up, don't we?"

"Thank you, Mr. Tate," Carol Anne replied, turning a shade of red.

"And this is Ryc," Jenn said, changing the air once more.

"I've heard a lot about you," Mr. Tate said, offering me his hand as well. "Jenn was right about you looking like one of the Osmond brothers."

"Is that good or bad?" I asked, shaking his hand.

"As crazy as she is about Donny Osmond," he smiled. "I would tend to think that it was very good."

She was crazy about Donny Osmond. Her bedroom walls were covered with pictures and posters of him. It was okay, because I had my share of pictures on the wall in my room. My pictures were mostly of Goldie Hawn and Julie Andrews.

"Donny Osmond, huh?"

"Yeah," Jenn laughed, hugging up to me. "I wouldn't be surprised if you didn't have a star crush of your own."

"Maybe," I said, laughing with her.

"He has it bad for Goldie Hawn and Elvis," Carol Anne said.

"Goldie Hawn, huh?"

"I like her eyes and the way she laughs," I confessed.

"Are you staying for lunch?" Mr. Tate asked Carol Anne, as we were walking back up to the house.

"No," she replied. "I have to go into Parsons with my folks, to pickup supplies. We just got back from Memphis a few days ago, and don't have a thing in the house."

"Maybe next time," he offered.

"Sure," she smiled, and turned her attention toward Jenn and me. "I'll catch-up to you guys later, okay?"

"Okay," I said, and watched her walk away.

Like myself, I knew she felt out of place. Maybe even more so, and that caused me to feel for her even more. I didn't say anything, because I suddenly felt like I was in the middle of something I didn't really want to be in. Something I honestly didn't have a clue to, or how to even get out of.

"Are you, okay?" Jenn asked, as we sat down on the deck to wait for her father to fix our lunch.

"Yeah," I lied. "Why do you ask?"

"Carol Anne," she replied, looking me dead in the eyes.

"Carol Anne is my best friend," I stated. "I know she felt out of place being with us, and I guess I kind of feel for her."

"I see," Jenn said, and sat back in her seat. "Just how close are the two of you?"

"I don't know," I said, because at the moment I wasn't really sure.

"Have you guys ever. . ."

"Messed around?" I asked, finishing the statement for her.

"Yeah," she replied.

"No," I said. "It's not that kind of relationship."

"Then what kind of relationship is it?"

"The kind that goes beyond the expression of simple words," I replied, because that was the truth that I believed. "She's the one friend in the world that I would trust with my life, or even die for."

"I've never had a friendship like that," Jenn said, and I knew she was starting to understand what I didn't know how to say. "I envy that with a desire to want to call it my own."

"Thank you," I said, taking her hand into mine. "I wouldn't feel right if you thought Carol Anne would try to come between us. Besides, my relationship with you, is on a higher plane than the one I share with her."

"Thanks," she smiled. "Anyone would be lucky to have a friend like you. You're honestly one of a kind."

"I'm not that special," I said. "But thank you anyway."

"Jennifer tells me that you write songs," Mr. Tate said, bringing a tray of drinks out. "Do you sing as well?"

"I play around with it," I replied.

"Is that your goal in life?" he asked. "To become a recording artist?"

"One of them," I said. "I haven't really taken the time to think about long range goals yet. I would like to see what my options are first."

"You have plenty of time for that," he smiled. "Feel the waters of high school first, and then think about your goals."

"I'll do that," I said, reaching for a can of soda.

"You sound like you have a good head on your shoulders," he said.

"Tell my Dad that," I smiled.

"Daddy?" Jenn said, holding her nose.

"Hang on, Honey," he said, and I saw that her nose was bleeding.

"Are you, okay?" I asked, as he went around to help her.

"Yeah," she said, behind a hand full of blood. "When I get too hot, I get some really bad nose bleeds."

"I've been there before," I said, and watched her Dad take care of it, as if it were something he did on a regular basis.

The rest of the afternoon took off better than I had originally anticipated. We ate our lunch, and talked about living in Tennessee. There was no more talk about Carol Anne, or the nose bleeds. In the back of my mind, I knew the thing with Carol Anne wasn't over. Things like that just don't go away.

Especially, with girls.

Only time would tell the rest of the story. A story I was going to try not to get too wrapped up in. Mostly, because I was already in over my head. It was something I didn't quite understand, and that bothered me.

I mean, why me? Why Richart Drake Lewis? What was the attraction both these girls saw in me? Back home in Indiana, girls like these two would have never given me a second look. So, what was the deal? What did they see in me that I didn't see in myself?

I ain't nothin' but a wanna be.

A nobody dude, with a handful of songs, and no promises to offer.

It just didn't fit into the scheme of things. At least not anything I knew. Being in love was something that was more like a dream I never believed I would find. Especially, with girls like Jenn and Carol Anne.

What was the deal? What was the deal with those nose bleeds? It seemed like a normal event to them, while it was happening. An event that went without further conversation, once it was under control. But then, who really wants to talk about a nosebleed?

Maybe it was just me. Maybe people really do have nosebleeds like that. How was I to know? I'm not a doctor.

I'm just a punk kid, with a guitar. Hell, that's more than likely all that I'll ever be. A nobody with a nobody future.

# CHAPTER ELEVEN

CAROL ANNE AND I were into some really heavy kissing, when she sat up on me, and pulled off her white tank top. Her bare breasts greeted me with points standing up, firm and high. I had not intended this to go that far, and was somewhat surprised that it had.

Carol Anne and Ryc, best friends and all, were no longer what we claimed to be. We had crossed over the line, and for a few moments we froze within that unspoken thought. Neither one of us was sure where we were headed, and that scared me.

Slowly, I reached up, and touched her erect nipples with my trembling fingers. In the back of my mind, I could hear Conway Twitty singing, "You've Never Been This Far Before." He was right. Neither one of us had ever been that far before. In the background of the song playing in my head, I could hear my Dad's voice telling me the dangers of getting that close to a girl, and what would happen if I went too far.

Still staring into each other's eyes, she lowered her mouth to mine, and started kissing me passionately. I returned the kisses, with the same passion, and hunger she was drowning me with. Dad's little story, about the thing in my pants taking control of the moment, kept getting louder and louder in my mind. It was doing exactly what he warned me it would do.

"Ryc?" Carol Anne called, from the bedroom window. "Are you awake?"

I opened my eyes to a sudden rush, and realized I had been dreaming about Carol Anne and I caught in the temptations of love. Why? I asked myself. Was I secretly in love with her? I wasn't for sure what was going on at the moment. The only thing I was sure of, was that the dreamed seemed so real, and I knew I was starting to press my luck.

Especially, when I looked out the window, and saw that Carol Anne was dressed exactly the way she had been in my dream. Was the dream a foreshadow of things to come? Was it trying to tell me that the two of us were on the way to crossing the line?

Whatever it was, I suddenly found myself not sure I could trust myself alone with her. That was a feeling I didn't like. A feeling that told me exactly what the dream was trying to tell me. Our lives, our little corner of the world was about to change.

The question was how?

The other question was when?

"Carol Anne?" I questioned, in low tone. "What are you doing here?"

"I need to talk to you," she whispered back. "Can we go for a walk?"

"Yeah," I replied, thinking that my bedroom was the last place we wanted to be. "Let me get dressed first."

When I pulled the covers off, I noticed that a part of the dream was still hanging on, and I kind of panicked. I quickly turned my back to her, hoping she had not seen what I saw. If she had, I would have been totally embarrassed beyond anything I have yet to know.

"Are you, okay?" she asked.

"Yeah," I choked. "What do you need to talk about?"

"Us," she whispered, as I was making my way to the window.

"Where do you want go?" I asked, once I was out side.

"To the Thinking Rock," she replied. "No one will bother us there."

"Okay," I said, and off we went.

Neither one of us spoke a word, until we were well out of sight of the house. My mind, however, wouldn't shut up. I kept thinking about how real the dream was, and wondering what it was all about. I felt really nervous being alone with her, thinking that anything could happen. Thinking that I was going to get myself into trouble, and that I wasn't sure that I could stop myself from letting it happen.

"I can't deal with this anymore," she said. "I can't sleep, I can't eat, and I can't stop thinking about the way I feel."

"How do you feel?" I asked, thinking it was a stupid question to ask.

"I love you," she said. "I love you, and I'm jealous of you and Jenn."

"I thought that it might be something like that," I said, not knowing what else to say.

"The thing is," she said, and I could tell she was crying. "I love Jenn too. She's my best friend, and I don't want to come between all of us."

"I would have trouble sleeping with all that on my mind too." I said. "Any ideas what to do about it?"

"Yeah," she said. "As much as I hate to say this, I think I'm gonna see if I can go back to my aunt's for a while."

"Are you sure?" I asked, hating the idea that she might be leaving me again.

"Yes," she replied. "I've given it a lot of thought, and feel that it might be what I need to get over my jealousy of you and Jenn."

"It might make it worse," I warned.

"I hope not," she said.

"What if I told you that I didn't want you to go?" I asked, not believing I had said it.

"All the more reason I should go," she said. "Being around you only makes it harder to deal with. What we share as friends should never be broken, or taken for granted. It should be cherished, and up held."

That made me feel really bad, about having the dream. It also, made me feel like the changes we were headed for, was because of this unspoken dream. A dream that I would never tell her about. No matter how the end turned out.

"You're starting to sound like me," I said.

"We're one in the same," she smiled, and wiped away some of her tears.

"I'm gonna miss you," I said, with tears of my own starting to fall.

I hated the moment we were in. I hated not being able to make it any better. I hated the idea of change, and losing a very important part of myself.

I hated knowing that somewhere in my heart, I loved her the same way she loved me. Like her, the problem was, I didn't want to come between the three of us. I was just as deeply in love with Jenn, and that confused the hell out of me.

Guess you can't have your cake, and eat it too.

"I'm so afraid that things are gonna change between us," she said. "That all we've try to save has been a waste of time."

"That's the saddest part of all," I said "Knowing that love has already changed us beyond the point of truly holding on to our magic."

"I know," she said, as a new flood of tears came.

"That doesn't mean I want to stop trying," I said, wiping away a few of the tears.

"I love you," she said, holding my hand to the side of her face.

"I love you too," I whispered, but she didn't hear me. She had taken off, right after tellin me, because there was nothing else that could be as important as those words.

Our lives were changing faster than a speeding bullet. What we were to each other, what we tried so very hard to save, were fading away. We would never be the same friends we once were, and that was a crime in itself.

A crime love had seen fit to commit, and rob away from us.

## CHAPTER TWELVE

"WHAT KIND OF DREAMS do you have, Ryc?" Jenn asked, as we were kicking sand on the beach down from her house.

"My Mom thinks that I should study art and become an artist," I said, without looking at her. "While my Dad thinks I need to get a real job, because he doesn't think I'll get anywhere as an artist."

"Yeah," she said. "But what does Ryc want to do?"

"I want to write," I said, as she took my hand into hers. "I want to write my songs for the world. It doesn't matter if I make it as a singer or not, just as long as I can write the things I feel."

"I never knew you were an artist," she said.

"I'd rather be a writer," I smiled. "Even though I'm probably a better artist than I'm a writer, and that's okay."

"What kind of art do you do?"

"Mostly I draw people," I replied. "Someday I'd like to try my hand at oil painting, but I've just not been able to yet."

"You know you can be anything you want to be, don't you?" she asked, and squeezed my fingers in her hand.

"Yeah, I know," I said. "It's just that in the world I live in no one ever takes the time to notice."

"I would," she said.

"Thanks," I said back to her. "The thing is, I ain't nobody, Jenn. I ain't never gonna be nothin' more than Ryc Lewis."

"If you keep believin' that way," she said. "That's all you're ever gonna be in the eyes of the world."

"It's not me," I defended. "It's the people in my life that's gonna hold me back. The people I love and care about."

"You won't always be with these people," she said. "If you allow yourself the chance, one of these days you're gonna open your eyes, and ride outta here on the first wind that comes along."

"You really think so?"

"Yeah, I do," she smiled. "I'm also gonna be the one holdin' onto your coat tail when that time comes."

"Man," I laughed. "And I thought I was the dreamer."

"You've got to have a dream in order to make it real," she said. "Sometimes it takes a long, long time to become real. You're just getting to the point where you're giving yourself something to think about. When you're ready, you'll know you're ready, and then you'll make it happen."

"Maybe I will," I said, as we walked onto her house.

She was right. How could she not be?

We all choose the paths we walk, unless we let others do it for us. With Jenn in my corner, I knew I couldn't possibly go wrong. I didn't know how long it would take me to get to where I wanted to be, because I was just starting to dream, and that was my biggest problem. She believed in me, and that was enough to know that one day so would I.

Only God and time knew exactly when.

"You know," I said, at the bottom of the steps that lead up to her house. "Sometimes I feel like Jim Stark in 'Rebel Without a Cause."

"Why's that?" she asked.

"His relationship with his parents," I replied. "Only mine's turned around from his."

"Makes you want to explode, don't it?"

"It makes me think that one day I just might," I said. "I might be an old man when it does, but once it does the whole world is gonna know who I am, and they won't ever forget either."

"You sound more like James Dean than Jim Stark," she smiled, with a little laugh to hide the seriousness of it.

"Maybe," I smiled, with the same gesture.

"Maybe hell," she said. "You've just not figured out what your cause is yet."

Man was that ever true. With everything that was trying to take place in my life at the moment I didn't have time to think about what I really wanted, and more than likely not for sometime to come. I was too damn busy trying to figure out everything else for that to happen.

I knew these things would eventually figure themselves out with or without me. But like my Momma, I'm a worrier, and that made it all the much harder.

You might say that my eyes were still closed, and probably would be for sometime to come.

Hopefully that was the answer.

## CHAPTER THIRTEEN

I WAS SITTING IN my room, later in the day, when my Dad came home from a visit to Uncle Pete's. By the way he slammed the door of his truck, I knew that he was upset about something. Something I knew I wasn't going to want to know.

"Ryc?" he called, when he came into the house.

"He's in his room," Mom told him, as I heard his footsteps coming down the hall.

"I want to talk to you about something I was told today," he said, shutting my mother out in the hallway.

"What?" I asked.

"Your cousin Debbi told her Dad that she saw you kissing that Oddley girl," he replied, turning really red in the face.

"It wasn't what Debbi thought it was," I stated.

"Then what do you call kissing a girl?" he asked, turning even redder.

"She was just showing me how to kiss," I confessed. "Is there a crime in that, or does your way of thinking say it was something else?"

"Don't get smart with me," he snapped.

"I'm not trying to," I said.

"Then explain to me why she would have to do something like that?" He demanded, in a tone that told me he wasn't gonna buy anything I told him.

"Because I've never been kissed before," I replied. "Is it all that wrong for her to show me how, or do you think I should just know how to do it?"

"I told you not to get smart with me," he snapped again. "And yes, kissing a girl the way I was told you were supposedly kissing her can lead to other things."

"It's not like that with Carol Anne and me," I said, wondering if I were lying about it or not?

"We're best friends, and both of us know that a love relationship like that would only destroy what we share now."

That part was the truth.

"I'm not buying it," he said. "As a matter of fact, I think the two of you should stop spending so much time together."

"You can't stop me from seeing my friends," I said. "That wouldn't be fair to me or her."

"Watch me," he snapped, and stormed out of my room.

Dad was a real son of a bitch at times. It kind of made me hate being around him. He had his own way of thinking, and never cared to hear what I had to say.

At least not when I was telling the truth.

"Dad," I cried, running after him. "Leave Carol Anne out of this. It's not about her. It's about what you think about me."

"I can't do that," he said, opening the front door. "The two of you have already crossed the line as far as I'm concerned."

"Dad," I cried again. "We're not doing anything wrong."

"Don't push it," he snapped.

"Don't push what?" I asked, and grabbed him by the arm.

Big mistake.

He grabbed me by the shirt, and threw me over the sofa, and into the wall. I tried to get up, but he was on me before I could, and threw me across the room into the front door. When he was mad, he was mad, and this was one of those times.

"Jim," Mom screamed.

"Leave it alone, Jane," Dad said, giving her a hard look. "He's been asking for this every since we got to Tennessee."

"If you hit me," I said, picking myself up off the floor. "You'll never hit anyone else."

"Right," he said, then hit me so hard my lights went out, so quick I didn't have time to see the stars.

Mom and my two little brothers apparently helped me to my room, where I woke up an hour or so later. Dad was nowhere to be seen. Which usually meant, he got so mad at himself, he took off to get drunk.

I was right. He came home later in the evening, drunk on his face. That meant, that I was more than likely gonna get some of the same abuse.

"I did it," he yelled, beating on my bedroom door. "You and your girlfriend are not allowed to see each other for the rest of the summer."

"Why?" I asked, from my side of the door.

"Because you're just a punk kid, with a hard on," he laughed. "You'll just have to do your guitar instead."

"I hate you," I said, but not loud enough for him to hear.

I just didn't want to deal with him, or face him any more that night. Not to mention the fact that I didn't want him to hit me anymore. I was still trying to get over the last blow he hit me with, to deal with anymore.

I had never hit him, or even tried to hit him in the past. Yet, I felt I was starting to get pushed to that point, and to tell you the truth, it scared the hell out of me. Actually, I think I was more scared of what I might do once I did start fighting back.

Mom came in later, after he had past out, and told me that he had done what he said he was going to do. He went over and had a talk with Carol Anne's Dad, who agreed with him that maybe there was more to our friendship that either one of us knew. With that forged into their thick skulls, they forbade us to see each other for the rest of the summer.

Dad had no right to judge us by his own ideas. He wasn't us. He didn't know how we felt, how we believed, or even how we were working our problems out. He only knew the way he was when he was my age, and that wasn't fair for me to be judged by.

He just couldn't get it through his head that I wasn't him, and that I never would be. Even with the problems I was facing, I still was a better man than he was.

But then, I was puzzled by the fact that his fears were becoming a reality. I hated it beyond any measure of the word, because I knew he would never see who I really was. He would never give me the chance to prove it, and that just wasn't fair.

Nothing was. Nothing ever was.

Sometimes I wonder, if what I was going through, wasn't because of the things he was putting me through. That maybe I was going through some kind of rebel act, or a get even scheme just to make him happy he was right. If I was, what would that make me? Just like him?

Oh, God, I hope not.

## CHAPTER FOURTEEN

"DID YOU EVER HAVE one of those problems with girls that you just couldn't figure out?" I asked Roy Miller, as we were taking a break from riding, at the Floating Store.

"Not really," he confessed. "They either like me, or don't."

"You have had a girlfriend, right?"

"Yeah," he said. "As a matter of fact, I've been trying to win her heart back for days now."

"Who is this mystery girl?"

"Kitty Steward," he replied, with a smile.

"You're the guy," I laughed.

"What do you mean?" he asked, looking real surprised. "Do you know her?"

"I know of her," I said. "I over heard my cousin and Carol Anne talking about her and this guy she broke up with last summer."

"What did they say?" he asked.

"They said you were acting crazy around some other girls," I replied. "And that she thought you were flirting with them."

The true story, according to the girls was, Miss Kitty Steward caught him in a lip lock with another girl. I didn't want to bring up any hard memories, so I faked it for thirty bars. Also, because he was my friend, and I didn't want to come across like I was cutting him down.

"That's almost right," he said. "The truth is, I was caught kissing this other girl, who was actually kissing me. I just didn't fight her off."

"Bad move," I said, realizing I was somewhat in the same boat.

"What's this deal with you?" he asked. "And are they the same two girls?"

"Yeah," I said. "The question I would like to know is, what if the two girls are best friends, and both of them are saying they're in love with you?"

"Shoot yourself," he replied.

"I already thought of that," I laughed. "But then, I figured if I did that, they would end up following me, and I would have to deal with it for all eternity."

"That's deep," Roy said. "I hope I never fall into those kind of shoes."

"You're saying you can't help me. Right?"

"Which one of them do you like the most?" he asked.

"That's the problem," I replied. "I like both of them the same. One's my best friend, and the other one I'm actually going with."

"Does she know your friend and hers, has the hots for you?"

"No," I stated. "She thinks we're just really close friends."

"Lyin' ain't good," he said. "That'll be the first grounds for both of them to leave you, and then you'll be stuck with ole lady thumb and her four daughters."

"Any ideas?" I asked.

"Does the other one, the best friend, know you're going with the one you're going with?"

"Yes," I said.

"Interesting," he said. "Which one puts out?"

"To tell you the truth," I said. "I think if I asked, they would both put out, as you say."

"Do they have any sisters?" Roy smiled.

"You're not helping," I stated.

"Okay," he said. "As hard as this maybe for you, I would stay with the one I was already going with."

"That's what I thought," I said. "I just didn't want to hurt the other one."

"Someone's gonna get hurt either way you go," he stated.

"That's the entire problem," I said. "Someone's gonna get hurt, and I'm the one that's gonna end up doing it."

"When you're hot, you're hot," Roy winked. "The only thing I would like to know is, how can two good lookin' babes . . . I hope they're good lookin'. . . be in love with your ugly mug?"

"I keep asking myself the same question," I replied.

"What kind of answer is that?"

"When you're hot, you're hot," I replied, and we both started laughing.

"I'm gonna tell you like it is," he said, really serious like. "Either you break it off with one of them, or they're gonna break it off with you."

That was the plain and simple truth to it. The problem was, I didn't know how to do it, with either one of them. Each day brought me closer and closer to both of them, and made it harder and harder to think about. Especially, with the new and confused feelings I was starting to have for Carol Anne.

It was like riding a roller coaster, staying on top, and looking down. Knowing that there weren't any breaks that you could see, once you did get started. There wasn't anyway off either, once it started. It was straight down, with a speeding rush, and hoping it would come to a satisfied end.

The thought of it shook me to the very core of my soul. I was in love with both girls, and didn't want to have to make a choice. That's right. I was in love with both of the girls, and pretending not to be. Facing up to that, I guess, deserved me getting blown out of the water, or knocked down a few notches. It wouldn't be fun, but then, falling never is.

Besides, Carol Anne was already being hurt by it all. She was hurt because she didn't know what to do about her feelings, and I didn't know how to help her through it, without hurting Jenn in the process.

I was going to have to do something, by putting a stop to the madness. One way, or another, I had to decide what path I was going to take, and stick to it. I just wish I knew why I had to be the one to pull the trigger?

It wasn't fair. It wasn't fair to any of us.

Just when I was starting to feel like a king, and all the world around me was right, the kingdom became nothing more than a broken dream. But then, even kings fall from their thrones, once the fatal stone is cast. If I would have known all this in the beginning, I think I would have never fallen in love.

Then, there would be no throne to fall from.

# CHAPTER FIFTEEN

AFTER I TOLD JENN about what my Dad had done, we agreed to try not to let him see us together.

I didn't much care for the sneaking around stuff, but knew I didn't have another choice. In this case, I'd been really upset if he wouldn't let me see Jenn. So far, no one in the family knew about her, and that was the way I wanted to keep it.

I know it wasn't fair to Carol Anne, being the one to take the fall for what Jenn and I were to each other. Then again, Dad was half right about Carol Anne and me. If he only knew that I was really trying, maybe things would be different. At any rate, it let some of the pressure off of me, trying to solve my problem of which one to hurt.

If I could change the thing with my Dad, I would. He was just seeing too much of himself in me, to understand that I wasn't him. He just wouldn't listen to reason, so there was no need for me to try at this point. Carol Anne and I would just have to not see each other for a while.

Dad was always final in his choices. It was either his way, or his way. That's how it had always been, and more than likely how it was always gonna be. My Dad knew it all, and never ever once let us forget that he did.

Once we started school, he couldn't do anything about it. Then again, I would be back to the point of having to decide what I was gonna do? Who I was gonna hurt?

So why couldn't I get Carol Anne off my mind? Why couldn't I talk to Jenn about that part of it, and see if she could help me? Why? Because then, she would be the one pulling the trigger. We'd breakup, I still wouldn't be able to see Carol Anne, and the king would have finally taken his fall from top his piece of cake.

"What is this?" Donny Long said, pulling up beside Jenn and me, as we were walking to the Floating Store.

"What's what?" I asked, realizing that his girlfriend, (my cousin) was the one responsible for my sneaking around, and my not being able to see Carol Anne.

"Mr. Hot-pants, has two girlfriends," Donny replied, smiling one of those grins you just hated to look at. "Now ain't that something?"

"What's he talking about?" Jenn asked.

"He hasn't told you?" asked Donny. "Why would he tell you?"

"Tell me what?" Jenn asked, with an upset look in her eyes.

"He's my cousin Debbi's boyfriend," I replied. "He and my cousin, saw Carol Anne and I walking together the other day."

"And did we see them together," Donny smiled the same hated smile.

You could tell he was enjoying this. That in itself, was just a little more than I could handle. With all the other things going on, he's lucky I hadn't broke.

"What do you mean?" Jenn asked, staring at me with fire in her eyes.

"Kissing like they were doing it all over the place," Donny said, and looked at me with one of those "get out of it" looks.

"Kissing?" Jenn asked, and I knew it was over.

"I'll explain," I said.

"Really," she replied. "You already seemed to have left that part out of your story, Ryc."

"She was showing me how to kiss," I said. "So that I would know how to kiss you, when the right moment came up."

"Why would she have to do that?" Jenn asked, with her hands on her hips.

"Because I've never kissed a girl before," I said, embarrassed I had to say it in front of Mr. Asshole. "Besides, she's my best friend, and there was no harm done."

"I could have shown you," Jenn said, a little more relaxed.

"I didn't want you to think I didn't know what I was doing," I confessed. "This is embarrassing enough."

"Well, Sweet Cakes," Donny said. "If you're done with the loser, I'd be more than glad to take over. A babe that looks as hot as you, needs a good man, to keep her happy."

"Don't you have a girlfriend?" Jenn asked, with one of those "if looks could kill" looks.

"Not if you're in need," Donny smiled.

"Don't push it, Long," I said, with my anger just reaching the point of over load.

"You want to make something of it, Dork?" Donny asked, and opened the door of his truck, to step out.

"If that's what it takes?" I replied.

"I wouldn't if I were you," Jenn said. "Ryc's a third degree black belt."

"Really," Donny said, sizing me up, and stopping in his tracks.

"Ask your girlfriend," Jenn smiled. "She'll tell you all you need to know about Ryc's fighting skills."

"How 'bout it, Dork?" he asked, looking at me. "Is she telling me the truth?"

"I'm still here, ain't I?"

"Okay," he said, climbing back into his truck. "I'm gonna check this out."

"You do that," I said, still standing in the same place I was, when this started.

"If I find out, this is a joke," he said. "I'm coming back to finish this."

"Anytime," I said.

"That's right," he said, and started his truck. "This ain't over, Kung Fu."

"Fair enough," I replied, staring into his eyes.

"Last chance, Sweetheart," he said to Jenn. "I'm more than you can handle."

"I'd rather do myself," Jenn smiled, and put her hands on my shoulders.

"Your loss," he said, pulling away, with his middle finger in the air.

"Why'd you tell him that black belt stuff?" I asked, as we continued to walk toward her house.

"Because he's a self-made jerk," she said. "And I don't like pricks like that."

"He's gonna want to kill me," I said.

"Don't you know how to fight?" she asked, and I could tell she was thinking about the kiss Carol Anne and I shared.

"Sure I do," I said. "As a matter of fact, I am into martial arts, and believe I could have taken him."

"Good," she said. "Now tell me about this kiss."

She had no way of knowing just how much I was into the arts, and that I really wasn't afraid to fight him. I wasn't a third degree black belt, or anything that extreme. I just knew a lot of moves, and wasn't afraid to fight. Martial arts was a secret hobby of mine that came about one day when I discovered that I had Chinese blood in me. It seems that back during the civil war, one of my direct ancestors, the second person in my family history to carry my name, (I'm the fourth) married a servant girl from China named Maelee. My family knew that I read books, and that I practiced the art. They just never knew how good I was, or how sincere I was to the art. That's mostly because I never had any formal training, or had ever been belt tested.

My family couldn't afford to send me, anyway.

"There was nothing to it," I said, and began telling her the complete story. Leaving out the part where I knew Carol Anne was in love with me.

"Poor Carol Anne," Jenn said, putting her hand into mine, after I had finished telling her the story. "She has to pay for our love."

"I know," I said. "It's not fair. Besides, there's nothing we can do about it, right now."

"Kiss me," Jenn said.

"What?" I asked, making sure that I had heard her right.

"Kiss me," she repeated. "I want to know how well Carol Anne taught you."

"Is that the only reason?" I asked, taking her into my arms.

"No," she smiled. "I want you to kiss me, because I love you."

I looked her straight in the eyes, cupped her face in my hands, and placed my lips gently upon hers. I don't know if it were fireworks, or if the sea had parted, or if time just stood still for that moment. What I did know was, I had never been kissed, until that moment.

It was one of those things you took inside your heart, and cherished for all the rest of your life. It was something you wouldn't ever forget.

It was what forever was made of.

# CHAPTER SIXTEEN

CAROL ANNE CAME OVER the next day, around ten in the morning. She looked like she hadn't slept in days. My Mom met her at the front door, before I could get there, and sneak her into my bedroom.

"Hi, Mrs. Lewis." Carol Anne said. "May I speak to Ryc?"

"You know you're not supposed to be around each other, don't you?" Mom asked.

"Yes," Carol Anne replied. "It's just that it's really important that I talk to him. I promise. There won't be any trouble."

"I thought that the punishment his Dad gave, was a little overboard," Mom smiled. "His Dad's at work right now, so I guess it'll be okay. Just don't let Jim, or the boys know that I gave in."

"Thank you," Carol Anne said, and kissed Mom on the cheek. "Where are the boys at now?"

"They're off fishing with their Uncle Pete," Mom replied.

"I'll try to be gone before they get back," Carol Anne said.

"You look like the walking dead," I said, stepping out of the hallway to meet her.

"I feel like the walking dead," she smiled, a forced smile. "I haven't been able to sleep at all the last couple of days."

"Remind me not to upset you," I said, trying to add some humor to the moment.

"Don't upset me," she said, with a "do you got it" smile.

"What's the deal?" I asked, knowing full well what was up.

"Can we go for a walk?" she asked. "I mean. It would be a lesser chance we would get caught together, and upsetting your Dad again."

"Mom?" I called, knowing she already heard what we were saying.

"Only if you stay out of sight," Mom said.

"Thank you, Mrs. Lewis," Carol Anne said.

"Really, Mom," I said, and kissed her cheek. "Thanks for understanding."

"I try," she said, and we were out the door.

To keep things simple, we cut through the woods, and went straight to the Thinking Rock. It was far enough out of sight that no one we didn't want to see us would. She didn't say a word, until we got there.

"This is a lot harder than I thought it was gonna be," she said, and sat down on the rock formation.

"What?" I asked, with yet another smile.

"You know what I'm talking about," she said, and shot me a hard look.

"I'm sorry," I said, sitting down beside her. "I was just trying to be me."

"I know," she said, with tears welling up in her eyes. "Do you know what it's like trying to be the best friend of someone you're in love with? Someone you can't even be around because of that love?"

"I understand," I said, putting my arm around her shoulders.

"Don't get me wrong," she said, as the tears broke free from their dam. "I'm not trying to start anything, or cause any more trouble. It's just that I have all these crazy feelings inside of me, and I don't know what to do with them. How am I supposed to deal with that?"

"I'm gonna be perfectly honest with you," I said, pulling her into my chest. "I really am in love with Jenn."

"I know you are," she said, pressing into me.

"It's really funny," I said. "But lately I've been having the same feelings toward you."

"Good," she laughed. "At least now I know. I'm not freaking out alone."

"You've never been alone with me around," I said.

"I know," she replied, and hugged me a little tighter.

"We make a really good pair, don't we?"

"Yeah," she said, and sat up.

"You know," I said. "Jenn has already given me the third degree about us."

"Does she know?"

"No," I said, wiping my own eyes. "I think I've convinced her we're just really good friends, and that we share a very special relationship."

"You can say that again," she laughed.

"Okay," I smiled. "We share a very special relationship."

"I'm glad she thinks that," Carol Anne said, playing with her fingers. "Because I really don't want to hurt anybody, or come between the two of you."

"So why are we talking about this?" I asked, putting my hand over her dancing fingers.

"Because I have to talk to someone," she said, and started crying again. "You're my friend, and the only person I know who wouldn't betray me."

That one hit kind of hard, because in away I was already betraying her. Even though we were never actually going together, it still felt like my relationship with Jenn was betraying what I felt for Carol Anne, and with her.

"Yeah," I laughed, because what else could a heel do? "I'm also the reason you need someone to talk to."

"It's crazy, ain't it?" she laughed.

"It's okay," I said. "We'll deal with it."

"It would be so much easier if I could just hate you," she said, and looked into my eyes. "I mean. I don't know what I mean."

"If I knew the answer to that," I smiled. "We wouldn't be talking about it. I wish I could make it easier for all of us. Only it's not that easy. I'm torn between the way I feel about you, and the way I feel about Jenn."

"Let me ask you this," she said, turning to face me a little more straight on. "If Jenn had never come into the picture, do you think you and me. . ."

"We already are," I replied.

"I told you not to upset me," she said, with a snicker.

"Despite the way things are," I said, putting my hand to the side of her face. "I could, and would have fallen in love with you, the right way. Meaning, if I hadn't already gotten involved with Jenn."

"I told you, you were upsetting me," she smiled.

"I didn't mean to," I smiled back at her. "You're not going to kill me, are you?"

"That would solve everything," she laughed.

"Okay," I said. "Shoot me, and get it over with."

"You're not making this any easier," she said. "Being who you are, is who I fell in love with. You make me laugh, you make me cry, and you make me feel alive."

"That's what best friends are for," I said. "Besides, we all need to be just a little be weird."

"You never have a problem pulling that one off," she smiled. "You're the nuttiest person I've ever met."

"Thanks," I said, and lightly tapped her jaw, with my fist. "Do you feel any better about things?"

"No," she replied. "But I can probably deal with it a few more days."

"Or until you need to talk again," I added.

"Yeah," she said. "Or until I need to talk to you again."

"Well," I said. "You know where my bedroom window is."

"That I do," she said. "But to tell the truth, that's not a fair invitation."

"Neither is that smile you're wearing," I said.

I don't really know if it helped the problem, or if it made it any worse. What I do know, is that it felt really good to see both of us laughing, and being that open with each other. We were star-crossed lovers, who didn't really know a thing about the human race. It was all alien to us, and something we were just learning about being adult.

Seriously, how many people do you know like us? The kind who can talk about the kind of deal we were talking about. I mean, here we are best friends and all, head over heels in love with each other, dealing with the fact I'm in love with her best friend, and still getting along.

That's not right, is it?

I mean, it's crazy, ain't it?

# CHAPTER SEVENTEEN

"HOW'S THE GIRL PROBLEM going?" Roy asked, the next afternoon, after we had gone riding for a while.

"Worse," I replied. "My girlfriend still doesn't know that her best friend has the hots for me."

"I'm telling ya," he said. "You'd better hope she doesn't find out, before you can tell her. Otherwise, someone is gonna get really hurt by all this. Women's feelings are something you just don't want to mess around with."

"Believe me, I'm starting to learn that," I said. "The really weird part of it all is, my best friend and I are talking about how she feels about me."

"You're what?" he asked, as if he couldn't believe I said what I had. "That's crazy. You're walking on dangerous ground my friend."

"Don't I know it?" I replied. "It's just that I'm her best friend, and the only one she feels she can actually talk to about it."

"How does that make you feel?"

"Like I'm from another planet," I smiled. "It's all alien to me, and that has me feeling a bit out of place."

"I bet it does," he laughed. "I'm still glad I'm not in your shoes."

"To tell you the truth," I laughed, a long with him. "I kind of wish I wasn't in my shoes."

"Who is this best friend of yours?" he asked, after taking a drink of his soda.

"Carol Anne Oddley," I replied.

"Carol Anne Oddley," he repeated, like he couldn't believe that either. "Quiet, little, wallflower Carol Anne Oddley? I don't believe it."

"What's so hard to believe?" I asked.

"She never talks to anyone," he said. "Sure, she's really hot and all, but you get used to the idea she's not really there."

"She's not that way around me," I smiled. "Actually, she talks all the time."

"That's hard to believe," he said, shaking his head. "I'd never guessed it was her. Not in a in a million years. Who's the other babe?"

"Jennifer Tate," I said. "You're probably going to tell me that you know her to."

"I've never met her," he said. "But I've heard of her. I think she only comes down here in the summer, or something like that. She's from Canada, ain't she?"

"Yeah," I said. "Only this time, they're gonna stay."

"Have you decided which one you like the most?"

"I guess, it's about the same," I replied. "I'm just hung up on the idea that I'm gonna be the one that does the hurting."

"You could always become an old class Mormon," he offered, with a smile. "I hear they were allowed to have two wives."

"Wouldn't that be great?" I asked. "Only I have a feeling the two girls won't go for something like that."

"Then you're hopelessly in trouble," he said. "You're either else gonna have to break it off with one of them, or play it as far as you can."

"You're a big help," I said, sarcastically. "You know. I really want to find away to make it easy for all of us."

"Good luck," he said. "I ride my bike, play my bass, and talk about the girls I would like to do it with. You don't get headaches that way. If I could help you, I would. The only thing is, you're in a place that doesn't fit anything that's normal to me."

"You can say that last part again," I said, taking that lost feeling to heart. "It's not anything that's normal to me either."

"Okay," he smiled. "You're in a place that doesn't fit anything that's normal."

He was right. The state of mind I was in, wasn't normal. I was insane to think this could all work out, with no one getting hurt. Carol Anne was already hurt, and it was because of me. Which meant that I had to do something about it.

The only problem, was what?

What was I gonna do to make everything come out in tomorrow's wash? Seriously, what was I gonna do? Why was I the one who had to decide? Love and war really isn't fair at all. The only thing wrong with this picture was, it was all about being in love. The war part of it was what I was dealing with.

It wasn't going to be easy, no matter what way it went. Not for me, not for Carol Anne, and not for Jenn. Not for any of us. We were all headed some place we didn't want to be, and didn't know we were headed for. It's the way things worked, when they had no other answers. It's why someone almost always gets hurt.

The question was who? The who, was something I didn't want to know.

Sooner or later, just as sure as the sun was gonna come up in the morning, the answer was gonna make its self-known. Someone was gonna get really hurt by all this, and I was gonna be the one that was gonna hurt them. Me, the stupid ass that walked blindly into these two relationships, with his eyes wide shut.

Now would be a good time to move back to Indiana.

Really it would.

## · CHAPTER EIGHTEEN

"I HAVE SOMETHING I want to say to you," I said to Carol Anne, as we sat at the Thinking Rock.

We always seemed to end up there for one reason or another. Maybe it was because that's where we first met the year before, and somehow our minds had claimed it as our special place.

I didn't know which.

Anyway, it was the first real time we'd been alone since we decide it would be best for us just to remain friends. Being there together was quite by mistake, because I really didn't expect to run into her.

I'd taken my guitar down there to get away from the rest of the world, and to play without anyone getting in the way. Not long after she showed up like it was destined or some kind of wonderful like that.

"You sound serious," she said, and took a seat next to me.

"I wrote a song for you," I smiled.

"You wrote a song for me?" she asked, with both a bewildered and excited look in her eyes.

"Yeah," I said, leaning against the backrest part of the rock formation so I could play the song for her.

"Why?" she asked, searching my face for the truth.

"Because you're an important part of my life," I said. "I need you in it despite every thing that's going on between us."

"It's not easy for me being just your friend, Ryc," she said.

"Life ain't easy," I replied. "We just take what we can, and always hope for more. Sometimes it comes, most times it doesn't, and through it all we hold dear to what we know is true."

"Okay, okay, play the damn song for me," she said with a smile.

"You're lucky you smiled," I said. "Otherwise I'd have to make you wait awhile longer to hear it."

"Oh," she said, and punched me in the arm. "You make me so mad sometimes."

"Hey," I said. "That's my chord arm."

"You're lucky I held the punch," she said, and smiled again.

"Well, maybe this'll cheer you up," I said, and started strumming the chords.

"A likely story," she laughed.

"Girl, I want you to know
Girl, from my heart and soul
I'll always be your friend
Oh, until the very end
Cause I love you
Yeah, I love you
Girl, you're the one who understands me
Girl, you see what others don't see
You're forever in my heart
No matter how far apart
And I love you
Yeah, I love you
Girl, please don't cry
Girl, you know I'd never lie
Cause the one thing that's true
Girl, is you
And I love you
Yeah, I love you."

I saw the tears fall way before the song ever came to an end. She was bright eyed, excited, and full of a love she could not share. "How's that?" I asked.

"I love you too," she said, stood up, kissed me for a lingering moment, and the walked off toward her house.

What else was there that could be said that could mean as much as the words "I love you?" It was everything, and nothing at all. It was life.

Our lives.

## CHAPTER NINETEEN

I WAS OUT IN the front yard doing a martial art's workout, when Uncle Pete, and the girls pulled up. Vicky followed Uncle Pete into the house, while Debbi came out to where I was. I was kind of upset with her, and didn't really want to see her.

"What's going on?" she asked, and sat down on the ground near me.

"Not much, since you got me in trouble with my Dad," I replied.

"What do you mean?" she asked, a little confused.

"Telling you're Dad about seeing me kiss Carol Anne," I stated. "She's my best friend, and I'm not allowed to see her for the rest of the summer."

"I'm sorry," she said, and I could tell she meant it. "I heard something about it, but didn't get the entire scoop. As for telling Dad what I saw, I just thought it was kind of cool seeing you with a girl. Especially since you're normally the shy type and all."

"I understand," I said. "The only problem with it is, Dad thinks Carol Anne and I are doing it. If you know what I mean?"

"Do I?" she laughed. "My Dad thinks the same thing is going on with Donny and me. He caught us necking on the front porch, and all hell broke loose. We're not allowed to see each other for two weeks."

"That explains why he was hitting on Jenn," I said, sitting down next to her.

"Wait a minute," she said, all excited. "Who is Jenn?"

"Jenn's my girlfriend," I replied, in kind of a whisper, because Dad was in the house. "I don't want you to breathe a word of it to anyone. Especially, my Dad, or anyone that might let it slip to him."

"I won't," she said, smiling from ear to ear. "Now, what's this about Donny hitting on her?"

"We were walking down by the Floating Store the other day," I said. "When he pulled up in his truck. First he made a few rude remarks to me, like he always does, and then made a couple of out of line suggestions toward Jenn."

"I bet that pissed you off," she said.

"I contained myself," I smiled.

"So what happened?"

"I let him know not to push it," I replied. "He took it that I wanted to fight, or something, and started to get out of his truck."

"What stopped him?"

"Jenn told him that I was a third degree black belt," I said, with another smile.

"I knew he was a chicken, when it came down to it," Debbi said, shaking her head.

"Yeah," I said. "It sure made him have second thoughts."

"Still," Debbi said, laughing. "I bet with what you do know, you could have beaten him. It would serve him right, for even thinking he could cheat on me."

"I'll tell you how you can get even with him," I smiled, remembering how we told him to ask her to prove it.

"How?" She asked, with keen interest.

"He's going to ask you if it's true, about my being a third degree black belt," I informed her. "When he asks you, tell him that I'm not. Tell him that I don't know a thing about fighting."

"How's that gonna get me even with him?"

79

"If you don't mind him getting knocked around a little," I said. "He's sure to come after me, when he hears what you have to say about my fighting skills."

"I get it," she said, shaking her head in agreement. "It'll prove to him that he needs to think about what he's doing, when it comes to us."

"Exactly," I said.

"Well," she smiled again. "Hit him a few times for me."

"Sounds like you're on a down slide in your love life," I said. "Is there anything I can do?"

"No," she said. "He's a jerk, and I'm just figuring it out."

"That doesn't sound to promising."

"It isn't," she replied. "So, tell me about your Jenn."

"You promise not to let my Dad know?" I asked.

"I promise," she said, and I believed her. "If I had known, your Dad was going to act the way he did about you and Carol Anne, I would have never said anything to anyone."

"Okay," I said, and told her the entire story.

She couldn't wait to meet her, but knew it wouldn't be for a while yet, because her family was going to take a trip to Arkansas and Oklahoma for a couple of weeks. Uncle Pete was from Oklahoma, and had some family still out there. This time every year, just before school started, they took trips like that, and were gone for what seemed like an eternity.

Debbi and I went way back as friends go. Disregarding the fact that we weren't actually cousins. My mother and her mother grew up together in an orphanage in Tipton, Indiana, and somehow that made them sisters. Therefore, we were brought up thinking that we were cousins, and that's how it was between us.

We were cousins. No ifs, ands, or buts about it. We were and always would be family. In some weird way, having that knowledge is also what made us the best of friends.

Anyhow, once Debbi was told the entire story, she was all for the reasons I was keeping Jenn a secret from my Dad. She felt bad about what happened with Carol Anne and me, and said that she would try to make it right. Even if she had to lie.

As for her relationship with Donny, she could care less if they worked it out, or not. "He's a total jerk," she told me, and I believed her. Yet, somewhere deep inside, I knew it hurt her more than she would ever reveal. Like me, Debbi was a survivor, and she would survive this. If she didn't, she knew where a shoulder would be to hold her up, if she fell.

I always would be.

The funny thing about my relationship with Debbi was, my father never thought twice about it. It was like; it was okay for us to be close, but not with anyone else.

I wonder why?

I mean. We even slept in the same bed. Even at this age. So what was the difference? Why was it all right for us to do that? You know, I think parents make up the rules as they go, and hope we're stupid enough to buy it. I mean, when you lay the cards out on the table, and take a really hard look at the picture, you'll see what I mean.

Seriously, think about it. Take a really hard look at it, and tell me I'm not right.

I'm betting I'll win.

## CHAPTER TWENTY

"I NEED TO TAKE a break," Jenn said, after we had been out walking the trails.

"Sure," I said, and picked a grassy spot near the river.

I noticed that she was looking kind of ill earlier, and kept it to myself. A selfish act on my part I guess, because I didn't want to give up a single moment with her. If I had said anything, she might have decided to stay home, instead of hanging out with me.

"Are you, okay?" I asked, feeling a little guilty.

"Yeah," she said, and forced a smile. "It's just that I've been up North in the cool air so long that I'm finding it hard to get used to this Tennessee heat."

"You can say that again," I said. "The climate down here is a lot hotter than I'm used to myself."

"It sure is," she said, and lay back on the grass.

I sat there for a long moment, just staring at her, while her eyes were closed, and thinking that she was still the most beautiful girl I had ever seen. Without thinking about what I was doing, I brushed her hair out of her face, and lay down beside her.

"Still," she said, without opening her eyes. "It's still one of the most beautiful places in the world."

"Okay," I laughed. "I'll admit that it's beautiful down here. I just prefer it to be about seventy-five to eighty degrees, rather than always in the hundreds."

"Yeah," she whispered, and I noticed she was drifting off to sleep.

I decided, what the hell? What was it going to hurt? I kissed her lightly on the lips, put my head next to hers, and started drifting off myself.

"Ryc?" I heard her whisper, an hour or so later. "It's getting late, and we should be going."

"I must have dozed off," I said, sitting up beside her.

"Guess we were both tired from all that walking," she smiled.

"That," I replied. "And the heat really can take it out of a person."

"Guess so," she said, still smiling. "You know, we're gonna have to remember this spot."

"Why?" I asked, as we both stood up.

"It's our first bed together," she said, and kissed me. "Now, no matter what, we can never say we haven't slept together."

"I guess not," I said, as we continued on our way toward her house.

"Can I tell you something?" she asked, holding my hand ever so tight.

"You can tell me anything," I said, returning the hold.

"I love you," she said, stopping, and moving around in front of me.

"I love you too," I said, staring into her eyes.

We held the look for a few minutes, than fell into a breathless kiss. The kind of kiss that probably could have set off enough fireworks to set the entire state of Tennessee on fire, if it had been allowed to get out of control. I don't know if it's true or not, but when they say the earth moved beneath them, it sure as hell moved beneath me. If it didn't, then we just had an earthquake.

As funny as it sounds, she was right about the spot where we had laid. It was our first bed together I think maybe that's what being in love with her was all about. Holding onto the idea that it could last for as long as forever.

"Hey, Sweetheart," Mr. Tate called, from the deck, as we were walking up.

"Hi, Daddy," Jenn said, kissing him on the cheek.

"Where have you two been?" he asked, reaching out to shake my hand.

"You won't believe this," Jenn said, with a smile. "We were out walking the trails, when I got a little too hot. We stopped to take a break, and both of us fell a sleep."

"You what?" he asked, with a laugh.

"We fell a sleep," she said again.

"You're lucky you didn't run into a snake, or something worse," he laughed. "I could just picture the both of you waking up, with a snake beside you."

"I'd die," I confessed.

"With me right behind you," Jenn laughed.

"Are you feeling okay?" Mr. Tate asked, reaching up to feel her head, with the back of his hand. "You still look a little peaked."

"I'm okay," she replied. "I just feel a little more than wore out."

"Maybe you should go in and take a nap," he suggested.

"I think I will," she said, and looked at me. "Is that okay, with you?"

"Sure it is," I replied, feeling a little out of place. "I probably should be getting home myself. My folks are probably wondering where I am anyway."

"Knowing a little bit about how parents work," Mr. Tate said. "You might not want to worry them too much."

"With my Dad," I said. "That's an understatement."

"See ya tomorrow?" Jenn asked.

"What time?"

"How about around noon?" she asked.

"Works for me," I said, and started off the deck.

"Hey," she said, coming over to where I was, and kissed me. "You're not getting away from me that easy."

I can't believe she did that, right in front of her father. Right in front of her father, and he didn't say anything. Man, I wish my Dad were more like that. Maybe then, things wouldn't be so damn hard on me. Hell, if all fathers were like that, there would be less trouble out of other kids in the world.

Not gonna happen.

"I'd never dream of it," I said, and kissed her back.

"Bye," she said, pressed up against me, with her arms around my neck.

"Bye," I said, and she kissed me again.

"See ya tomorrow," she said, and went back to her father's side.

"See ya," I said, and started on my way. "Have a nice evening, Mr. Tate."

"You too, Ryc," he said, and they both went into the house.

I was worried about her feeling ill. To tell you the truth, I was wondering about it a lot. Lately, she seemed to be down with something, or the other, and that didn't seem quite right. Of course, she could be right. Adjusting to the change in climate might be a little harder for her, and maybe it was the heat. Hell, like I said before, I'm no doctor.

I guess I'm a lot like my Mom, a worrywart. If we weren't worried about something, then there really would be something wrong. After awhile, you kind of get used to yourself, and just pass it off.

That's pretty much what I tried to do, because when I first came to Tennessee last year, there was a day or two that I felt sick myself. Guess we all take changes differently, when they come about, and this was really no different. Life was made up of changes that we go through every day, so you might as well get used to it. Then again, you could be a worrywart like me, and learn to let it pass in a Tennessee minute.

In a Tennessee minute, that sounds like a good title for a song. Think I'll go home, and try to lay the words down.

Sounds like the perfect thing to do.

"I'm gonna love you
Like you've never been loved before
I'm gonna love you
For now and ever more
Cause in a Tennessee minute
You're forever in it . . ."

## CHAPTER TWENTY-ONE

As I was walking home from Jenn's, I noticed Carol Anne walking toward me. She stopped. Leaned up against a tree, and waited for me. There was something in the way her eyes looked that caused alarms to go off inside my head. My heart rate picked up pace, and I suddenly became aware that I probably shouldn't be alone with her.

"Hey, Carol Anne," I said, knowing there was really no way out of talking to her.

"Hey," she said, in a softer than usual voice.

She was wearing blue jeans and a white tank top you could just almost see through. It made the feeling inside of me move to an attraction I wasn't sure I wanted to feel. The urge to get away from her as fast as I could, started to take hold, and made me feel a bit panicked.

"Where ya going?" she asked, stepping up to me.

"Home," I replied.

"Care if I walk with you?" she asked.

"I don't care," I said, because she still was my best friend and all. "Just don't let my Dad see us together. You know how he's been lately."

"I know," she replied, and we walked on a little. "Can I ask you something?"

"Sure," I said, trying really hard to not look at the front of her tank top.

"If Jenn hadn't come a long, do you think you and I might have considered going together?"

She asked, and I knew this was the feeling raging inside of me.

"You've already asked me that," I reminded her.

"I know," she said.

"Yeah," I said, answering the look in her eyes. "We might have considered it. Even though we were afraid that it might change our relationship."

"For good, or bad?" she asked.

"I would like to think that it would have been something good," I replied. "But then, that's something we'll never know."

"I bet it would have been for the good," she said, smiling at me. "Don't you?"

"Why are you still asking me this?"

"Because I have to know," she said, stepping in front of me. "Remember when I was showing you how to kiss?"

"I remember," I said, with her face only inches from mine.

"I was in love with you then," she said. "In fact, I've always been in love with you."

"What about your boyfriend in Memphis?"

"There isn't a boyfriend in Memphis," she confessed. "I was just trying to be cool."

"You should have told me the truth," I stated. "Maybe I'd come back here hoping for a relationship with you, and not gotten involved with Jenn."

"I was afraid I would lose you," she said. "Especially, if you knew how I really felt."

"I know what you mean," I confessed. "I've felt the same way."

"Kiss me," she said.

"I can't," I replied.

"Kiss me," she said again, and put her arms around my neck. "Kiss me, so I'll at least know what I've lost."

"It'll only make it worse." I said, with her nose brushing up against mine.

"I don't care," she said, as a single tear rolled down her cheek.

87

I looked at her for a very long moment, and was caught up in the magic of what was going on between us. A pure and natural innocent moment that could never be. I reached up, took her face into my hands, and kissed her.

It not only was torture for her, but it was equally as much torture for me. Especially, when she started kissing me back. I reached around behind her, took hold of her hips, and pulled her to me. The embrace was one of pure passion.

"We can't do this," I said, pulling away from her.

"I know," she said, and stepped back a few steps.

"I've got to go," I said, still feeling her pressed against me, in my imagination.

"Me too," she said.

"See ya," I said, brushing her hand, as I started to walk by her.

"I love you," she said.

"I know," I said, looking back at her, over my shoulder.

"See ya," she said.

"I love you," I said, knowing I shouldn't have.

We kissed each other one last time, and separated from each other in silence. There was nothing else that we could say, that could possibly mean as much. The moment had come and gone, and we would never talk about it again.

At least I hoped so.

We couldn't. I mean. How could we? It was a hopeless adventure we both knew that we couldn't take. Yet, ever step we took seemed to be bringing us that much closer to each other. We were slowly killing ourselves.

I was also in love with Jenn. I had already made a commitment by going with her. A commitment I couldn't just break. It was something I knew Carol Anne knew as well.

Yet, a part of both of us loved each other so much, we kept finding ourselves crossing the line, and now we were going to pay for it. It was torture. It was great. It was something we could never share again. Our friendship, our love for each other, would never allow it. No matter what the temptation was that crossed our path.

That's how reality would leave us, and it wasn't fair. It wasn't fair to anyone. It never would be. That my friend was life.

Really messed up.

# CHAPTER TWENTY-TWO

I HAD A LOT to think about. What was I doing? Letting it get out of control. That's what I was doing. Taking it to extremes that it should have never gone to. Extremes that would eventually destroy every thing that I wanted to keep.

I went into the house with my head in the clouds. Wondering what was happening to me? Thinking that I was becoming what my Dad had preached against, and hating every moment of it. Why couldn't I get the nerve to just let one of them go?

"Are you all right?" Mom asked, as we ate dinner.

"Yeah," I lied. There was no way I could let them know what I was dealing with.

"Is it that girl?" Dad asked.

"The one I can't see?" I asked, being a little out of line.

"Is there more?" he asked, with a surprised look.

"Only you would come up with a question like that," I said, getting up from the table.

"It was all for a good reason, Ryc," Dad said, staring at me.

"Who's? Mine or Yours?" I asked.

"You know what I mean," he said.

"Don't you think that I should be the one who gets to decide how my life is gonna go?" I asked. "Didn't you get to decide how your life went?"

"I made a lot of mistakes that I can't change," he replied. "Mistakes that I hoped you wouldn't make."

"They're my mistakes, Dad," I said. "I'd like to learn from them for myself."

He just kind of looked at me kind of stupid like, and didn't say a word. When you're right, you're right, and he knew I had made my point. I went to my room, without anyone saying another word. What could they say?

In my room, I sat against the headboard of my bed, hugging my guitar, with tears running down my face. It was all becoming more than I knew I could deal with, and that realization made it hurt even more. I didn't know what I was going to do.

I sat there, for what seemed like an eternity. Then without really thinking about it, I started strumming my guitar, as words appeared from out of the blue. Normally, that's not the way I write my songs. This one, however, came like it was born in a rage that would not let it be denied.

> "Thought that I didn't need anything
> To make it on my own
> But now I know I need something
> I can't make it alone
> You move me to no measure
> With a love so pure
> You're like a hidden treasure
> You're my only cure
> I love you, with a passion so close to pain
> I love you, like I love a walk in the rain
> I love you, with a passion so close to pain
> You're my only reason
> You're my only truth
> During the summer season
> Of my innocent youth
> You give me feelings I've never known

That comes with the raging wind
Feelings I've never shown
Because they're where I've never been
I love you, with a passion so close to pain
I love you, like I love a walk in the rain
I love you, with a passion so close to pain
I'm sorry I was so blind
I didn't know it was you
I was waiting to find
With a heart so true
There's a beauty in your eyes
That reaches out to me
Giving me the strength to realize
We were meant to be
I love you, with a passion so close to pain
I love you, like I love a walk in the rain
I love you, with a passion so close to pain."

When I finished, I knew I had been thinking about Carol Anne. She was the one that inspired my heart the most, and the one I needed to make my life complete. She was also the one I knew my Dad would never let me be with. What's that ole saying? "If you love something, let it go. . ." For the time being, that's what I had to do. I had to let Carol Anne go, and devote myself to my commitment with Jenn.

Wondering if there would ever be a time for Carol Anne and me.

"Ryc?" Dad called, from the other side of the door.

"Come in," I said, after wiping my eyes' dry.

"That was a very good song," he said, stepping in, and closing the door behind him. "What I heard of it. Is it one of yours?"

"Yeah," I said.

"Where do you get your ideas?"

"They just come to me," I said. "It's like a river running to the sea. When the song comes, the words keep on flowing."

"Do you write many love songs like that?"

"It's mostly what I do write," I said. "People tend to relate more to love songs, I think."

"They probably do," he smiled.

"Did you want something?" I asked, wondering why he was there.

"Not really," he said. "You just seemed a little distant tonight."

"My life isn't the same as it was yesterday," I said. "It's moving a head of me at warp speed, while I'm still trying to catch-up to when it started."

"It doesn't get any easier," he said.

"That much I've already figured out," I smiled.

"Tell you what," he said. "I'll give my punishment some thought, and let you know what I decide."

"Thanks," I said.

"Go to sleep," he said, opening the door. "You look like you could use some."

"Right after I write the words to the song I just played," I said. "I don't want to forget how it goes, in case I ever want to play it again."

"The way you remember things," he laughed. "I doubt that you ever would forget anything you came up with."

He was probably right, on that account. I rarely ever forgot anything I was told, or did. It was kind of like having a photographic memory. As good as it was it often got me in trouble. I tend to speak up about things that I shouldn't, always at the wrong time.

As for Dad, he sometimes really blew me away. This was one of those times, when he was in a rare good mood. Trying to figure him out was just as hard as trying to figure out the mess I was in. You rarely ever got anywhere with it.

I know I've said this before, because it's really the truth. It wasn't easy. Then again, there ain't nothing easy about living. It's either you do, or you don't.

I survive. One day, one step at a time.

It still ain't easy.

# CHAPTER TWENTY-THREE

ROY MILLER CAME OVER that week-
end, to stay all night, and to meet Jenn. Who wouldn't be home until
Sunday afternoon, when she got back from another trip to Nashville
with her father. Roy said that I was the first person his parents ever let
him spend the night with. That told me two things about them. One,
they were no different from mine. Two, they all had this over protec-
tive deal going on in their heads, that none of the teen-agers liked. A
sickness that I was sure would be catching up with all of us, once we
started having kids of our own.

"What are you boys planning to do tonight?" Dad asked us, Saturday afternoon.

"Nothing much," I replied. "We were thinking that maybe we would
watch Sir Cecil Creep, at midnight."

Sir Cecil Creep hosted the Saturday night horror flicks, and was a
favorite of ours. We were all lucky it was on one of the two stations we
could pickup out in the country.

"Good," he smiled. "You both can come with me. We'll be back in
plenty of time for you to watch Sir Cecil Creep."

"Okay," Roy and I said, at the same time.

I'm sure Roy didn't know what to make of it, any more than I did. He knew enough to know that we didn't want to get on his bad side either. Especially, after I had informed him of some of my mean Dad stories.

Much to our surprise, he took us to the Lexington Speedway. Where we got to watch hobby stock car races, at full speed, around a dirt track. The kicker to the event was the fact that Dad was driving a red '57 Chevy, with the number 007 painted on the side of it.

I knew that Dad had used to race, when I was a younger, but I didn't know he was still into it. It showed that I knew just about as much about him, as he claimed to know about me. It also explained where he was most Friday and Saturday nights. A secret that I'm sure if my Mom knew he was doing would either cause her to have a major heart attack, or her to beat him to death. The last I heard, she was totally against him racing anymore.

"Don't say anything to your Mom about this," he said, after coming in second in the big heap.

"We won't," I said. "But I would like to ask you a favor."

"What is this, some kind of blackmail?" he asked, with a smile.

"No," I replied. "It's just your son asking you to trust him on this issue."

"What?" he asked, with a bewildered look.

"I would like for you to let Carol Anne I start hanging out with each other again."

"I'll talk to her father," he said. "Let's go get us something cold to drink."

"Dad," I said.

"What?" he asked. "You sound serious. Is there something wrong?"

"No," I said. "I really would like for you to trust me on this."

"I'm trying," he said. "It's just not that easy sometimes."

"It never is," I replied.

"What do you want out of this deal?" he asked, looking at Roy.

"That's easy," Roy said. "I want to go for a spin in your race car."

"Damn," Dad laughed. "You guys are out for blood."

"Does that mean you're gonna take us?"

"Now what do you think?" Dad asked, and led us to the pit area.

It was a ride I'll never forget. We laughed at speeds up to eighty-five miles an hour, all the way around the track. The only thing I could figure out of all this was, Dad was either trying like he said he was, or Debbi had talked to him about what was going on. It didn't much matter at the moment, because we were all enjoying ourselves, and that was a good thing.

In reality, Dad wasn't all that bad. He just had a really bad side to him, that he seemed to always take out on me. It was the side I didn't like, but saw the most of. Mom said, that it had something to do with him being a diabetic, and that he sometimes didn't understand why he acted the way he did himself.

Only time would allow us to see the truth in each other.

If we survived that long.

# CHAPTER TWENTY-FOUR

                                    "ROY MEET JENN," I said. "Jenn meet
Roy."

"Hi," they both said, and shook hands.

"Who's this young man?" Mr. Tate said, walking into the room, with his briefcase.

"This is Roy Miller," I said. "He's one of my friends."

"Nice to meet you, Roy," he said.

"You too, Mr. Tate," Roy said, and shook his hand.

"What do you three have planned for today?" Mr. Tate asked.

"We're going to watch 'Rebel Without a Cause," Jenn said.

"James Dean," smiled Mr. Tate. "If I had known it was on, I wouldn't have made plans to go to Nashville today."

"Cancel," Jenn said.

"I would, Honey," he said, putting his arm around her shoulders. "But I can't. I have some big clients coming in, just for this meeting."

"Are you sure," she asked, with those eyes of hers.

"Unfortunately," he said, kissing her on the top of the head. "I would like you to tell me what you think of him. 'Rebel,' is my favorite of the three movies he starred in."

"Mine too," I said, with a smile.

"You've seen it before?" he asked.

"Yeah," I said. "My Mom made me stay up with her late one night, while we waited for my Dad to come in off the road."

"Ryc's Dad used to play basketball with him, when they were in school," Jenn said. "I think that's neat."

"Is that true?" Mr. Tate asked.

"According to my Dad it is," I replied.

"That is neat," he smiled. "Enjoy the movie, and I guess I'll see you when I get back."

"Okay, Dad," Jenn said. "I love you."

"I love you too," he said, and kissed her on the cheek. "Wanna walk me out to the car?"

"Sure," Jenn said, and then turned to Roy and me. "I'll be right back."

"I guess this makes you the man of the house, while I'm gone," he said. "Keep it together."

"Yes, Sir," I said, and they walked out to the car.

"Carol Anne is a good-looking girl," Roy said. "But Jenn is a total fox. If I were you, I think I would stay with her."

"You see where I'm at, don't you?" I said.

"Does Carol Anne know you made your choice yet?"

"No," I said. "I haven't seen her for a few days."

"Get it over with as soon as you can," Roy said. "If you don't, you're gonna regret it for the rest of your life."

"Regret what?" Jenn asked, walking back into the room.

"Roy thinks I should ask you to marry me," I said, with a smile, trying to cover myself, and lying at the same time.

"I'm not ready to get married yet," Jenn said. "But I'll be waiting for the day you do ask me."

"See, I told you," Roy said, going a long with me. "She'll marry you when the right time comes."

"What did you think of my Dad, Roy?" Jenn asked, changing the subject.

"He's kind of weird," Roy said.

"I like him that way," Jenn said.

"Me too," I added.

"It's the kind of weird I like," Roy said. "I didn't mean anything bad about it."

"It's okay," Jenn said.

"The movie doesn't start for an hour yet," I said. "Any ideas what we do until then?"

"Play one of your songs," Jenn suggested. "Seeing how I haven't heard one of them yet."

"Me either," chimed in Roy, who I think was starting to feel a little out of place.

"I don't have my guitar," I said, hoping to get out of it.

"We have a piano," Jenn smiled. "Plus, I have my drums."

"You play the drums?" I asked, with some surprise.

"Sure do," she smiled.

"Great," I said. "Roy plays the bass."

"Yeah," Roy said, with a bewildered look.

"The three of us can start our own band," I stated. "Wouldn't that be great?"

Roy looked at Jenn, Jenn looked at Roy, and then they both looked at me. Their mouths dropped to the floor in shock, and then into one of those "got ya" smiles.

"What's wrong?" I asked.

"We ain't starting anything," Jenn said. "Until we hear one of your songs."

"You heard what the lady said," Roy said, with a wink.

"This is what they call blackmail," I said, walking over to the piano. "Don't expect too much out of this, because I'm not that good at the keyboards."

"Just play the song," Roy said.

"Yeah, Ryc," Jenn said. "Play the song."

"Now you're ganging up on me," I said. "Give me a moment to warm up, and I'll play you one of my songs."

Aside from Carol Anne, no one has ever really wanted to hear me sing, or play my songs. Sure, my family could hear me playing at home, but they never came in to listen, or anything. The idea of doing it now, kind of scared me to death. It was a new experience I was going to have to get used to. Especially, if we were serious about this band idea.

That's when I started to play.

> "Outside the wind silently howls
> Speaking to its creatures of the night
> Calling them forth
> Into the beautiful ebony
> Dancing in the moonlight
> From stone to stone
> And feeling so alive
> In this chosen venue
> Where the night is so misjudged
> With its eternal beauty
> That is so often over looked
> By the fears of man
> And yet, us few
> Who dare to relish its magic?
> With a hunger few will ever know
> Because of that fear
> So here I reside
> From dusk 'til dawn
> With my own hunger
> That exists just the same."

They both just sat there, with their mouths open. I didn't know what to think. Did they like it, or not? They just sat there.

"Well?" I finally asked.

"What are we gonna call ourselves?" Roy asked.

"That was beautiful, Ryc," Jenn said. "It sounds like you're having a love affair with the night."

"You really think so?" I asked.

"Yes," she said.

"That's what I was trying to get across," I said. "To make people see that there is more to the night, than just the silly fears we have."

"You have away with words," Jenn said. "Away that really makes you feel what you're trying to say."

"Cool," I said. "By the way, the only love affair I'm having is with you."

"It better be," she smiled, and kissed me.

"So," Roy said. "What are we gonna call ourselves?"

That was the highlight of my day. I mean. I got to play one of my songs to people I've never played to before, they liked it, and we were gonna try to become a band. That meant that others would be getting to hear us play. It didn't matter to me if we made any money at it, at that point. It was more the thrill of just being able to do it.

Dreams like that only come a long every once in a while. When they do, you grab them by the horns, and take the ride. It doesn't matter how far you go, just as long as you go. Kind of like the mess I was having with Carol Anne and Jenn. It wasn't altogether right, it just was, and that was what I had to live with.

Aside from that, for once in my life, the world was right.

## CHAPTER TWENTY-FIVE

"Hey," Carol Anne called, from the road, as she made her way to the front porch. "How'd you get us paroled?"

"I cut a deal with my Dad," I replied.

"What kind of deal?" she asked, sitting down beside me.

"I asked him to trust me," I smiled.

"I hear you've got a band in the makings," she stated, reaching out to touch the strings on my guitar.

"Yeah, I do," I said, surprised that she had heard already. "Who told you?"

"Jenn," she smiled.

"You've been down to see her?" I asked, surprised at even that.

"She's my friend, you know," she replied looking at me.

"We need to talk," I said. "This thing between you and me, is driving me insane."

"I feel the same way," she said.

"Do you think we can put a hold on it?" I asked.

"I was gonna ask you the same thing," she said. "It's already costing us too much, if you know what I mean?"

"Yes," I said. "I know exactly what you mean."

"So," she said, changing the subject. "How's the band coming?"

I would love to believe that it was settled that easily, but that wasn't the way my luck was going lately. I had only to hope that it was, and wait until tomorrow to get the truth. It's the way it has always been, and you can't expect it to change just like that. Not with Carol Anne. Not with my Dad. Not with anyone. It just doesn't happen.

"We haven't actually played yet," I said. "It's still pretty much just an idea, but a working idea that has possibilities."

"You'll do just fine," Carol Anne smiled, and seemed like her old self. "Jenn invited me down to watch you practice. It's okay with you if I come, isn't it?"

"I'd love to have you there," I said. "It wouldn't be right if you weren't. Like, you were the first person I ever played anything for. Why wouldn't it be all right?"

"I just thought I'd better ask," she said. "With every thing else that has been going on between us."

"So what?" I asked. "We got romantic a few times. You and I are the very best of friends. You're a very important part of my life that I don't want to lose."

"I know," she said, with a very strong hint of tears. "I guess, I just needed you to remind me of it."

"If you look," I said. "You'll always find me, with my arms open wide."

"I love you for that," she said, and the tears fell.

"Hey," I said, and pulled her to me. "We don't let tears fall around here."

"I can't help it," she said.

"It doesn't work that way," I said.

"Okay," she said, and wiped her eyes. "Would you play me one of your songs, for old times sake?"

"Sure I will," I said, and started strumming.

> "I can't say enough
> To say what I have
> Because it's all that I am

In the words I write
My soul, my heart, my life
I would never lie to you
About something so true
That just wouldn't be me
I maybe an actor
Acting out the roles
I've encountered
Up until now
Because until now
I'm the only role
I've never played
But I'm playing it
For you. . ."

"You did it again," she said, wiping away more tears.

"What?" I asked.

"Put a smile on my face," she said, and kissed me lightly on the lips.

"That's what best friends do," I said, smiling back at her.

"You do it really well," she laughed.

"Then why are you crying?" I asked, wiping away a few of her tears, with my fingers.

"I don't know," she said.

"Well, stop it," I smiled. "You're gonna ruin my reputation."

"Okay," she said. "No more crying."

"Good," I said, and gave her a one-armed hug. "My songs aren't that bad, are they?"

"Would you give it up?" she asked, laughing so hard, she cried even more.

"Okay," I said. "How about going for a walk?"

"Where to?" she asked.

"Down the road," I replied. "One foot, one step in front of the other, and back home again."

"I'd like that," she said, as we walked off the porch into the cricket chirping sounds of the night.

It was true. Carol Anne was my best friend, and I did love her. I could honestly see her no other way, without losing something. She was a part of my soul, embedded in my heart for all of eternity. My life would have never been the way it is, if I had not known her.

I know she had other emotions she wanted to share with me, and I know she knew that it wasn't possible. In time, she would come to understand the way I saw her, and know that our bond was stronger because of it. It wouldn't be easy. Life wasn't that simple. It never was, and it never would be.

At least not the one I lived in.

Yet, it would be okay in the end. I would always be there to help her pickup the pieces when she fell. I would always have that shoulder for her to cry on. Just as she would always be there for me. That was the only true thing we knew about each other that mattered.

It was a special kind of love.

## CHAPTER TWENTY-SIX

I FACED MY REAL test the next afternoon, when Jenn and I were left alone at her house, and kind of got a first hand experience of what my Dad kept preaching about. It was one of those really hot days, when standing in the shade seemed just as hot as out of it.

"Would you like to go for a swim?" Jenn asked, as we sat in her room playing records.

"I don't know how to swim," I smiled.

"Neither do I," she said, with a laugh. "We could just go play in the water, and cool ourselves off?"

"I don't have any trunks," I said, really trying hard to get of it.

I hated the sight of my bare legs, and even worse the sight of me being shirtless. Why? Because for some unknown family secret, I was cursed with a lot of body hair.

"Dad won't mind if your borrow a pair of his trunks," she said.

"That's okay," I said, but she was out of the room, before I could come up with another excuse.

"I think these will work," she said, handing me a pair of black trunks.

"Are you sure you want to do this?" I asked.

"Sure I am," she said. "You can change in the bathroom, while I change in my room."

"Okay," I said, and stepped across the hall to the bathroom.

Well, I thought to myself. She's gonna see me that way sooner or later. I was just hoping that it would be a lot later.

"Are you ready?" she called, a few minutes later.

"Yeah," I said, stepping out of the bathroom. "Don't laugh at the way I look."

"I just love the sight of a hairy man," she said, rubbing her hands through my chest hair. "Besides, a little sun will do you some good."

"It'll probably make me burn," I smiled, feeling really awkward.

"It'll make you sexier," she said, and drug me outside.

Jenn, on the other hand, totally blew me away. She was wearing the same white bikini she was wearing the day I met her. Just so you'll get the picture, I'm gonna tell you one more time; she was still the most beautiful girl I had ever laid my eyes upon.

We chased each other around for several minutes, splashing, and throwing each other into the water. Making sure we didn't go out beyond the posted swimming area. She was right. It was a refreshing change, and just what we needed to cool ourselves off.

"What's wrong?" she asked, when we stopped to take a break.

I had noticed that when the top of her white bikini got wet, you could see her nipples, almost as if they weren't covered. She caught me looking, at the same time I noticed it, and embarrassed the hell out of me. I kind of felt like I was committing a crime of some kind.

"Did you know you were showing through your top?" I asked, realizing she probably already knew what was going on.

"Yeah," she said, biting her lower lip. "Most suits like this do. Is it a problem?"

"No," I said, looking away.

"You're embarrassed," she laughed, and gave me a hug that put us both down in the sand.

"It's just that I've never seen you like this before," I said, not knowing what else to say.

"It's okay," she said, kissing me, as she lay on top of me. "I won't tell, if you won't?"

"It's our secret," I said, rolling her beneath me, where it was my turn to kiss her.

"Let's go to the house," she said, staring into my eyes, with a suggestive look.

"Okay," I said, and raced her to the house.

I really didn't know what to expect, as we laughed all the way to the deck. I wasn't really expecting anything, if you know what I mean. Yet, for some strange reason, my Dad's voice started burning my ears. "If you get her knocked up," I heard him saying. "It's your baby, not mine."

It scared me. I didn't know if I could really trust myself not to do anything stupid. I loved this girl. If that was what this was going to lead to, would I be able to not go all the way? I couldn't really tell you. My heart was racing a million miles an hour, as she led me into the bathroom. My Dad's voice kept ringing in my ears, a little louder with each step we took.

Man, was I scared?

"Let's take a quick shower," she suggested. "To wash off the sand."

"Okay," I said, because there wasn't much else I could think of.

In the shower, we let the spray wash our bodies, and swimming suits clean of the Tennessee River. Facing each other, she put her arms around my neck, and pressed her body into mine. I put my trembling hands on her hips, and held her there. We were so close; I thought we could climb into each other's skin.

"I love you," she whispered, still staring into my eyes.

"I love you too," I said, pressing my lips to hers, in cool spray of the shower.

We stood there, kissing for what seemed like an eternity, when she suddenly stepped away from me, and removed her top. It was all as if it were the most natural thing in the world. I just stood there; watching her, and watching it fall to the floor.

"Touch me," she whispered, as she guided my trembling fingers to her breasts.

They felt soft and smooth. Her nipples went erect to my touch, and started to cause parts of my body to stir as well. She closed her eyes, pushed the lower part of her body into mine again, and wrapped her arms back around my neck. I lowered my hands to the lower part of her back, and started kissing where my hands had been only moments before.

As she was pushing my face into her breast, we both heard the sound of her father's car pulling into the drive, and looked at each other in total shock. Panic sat in really quick; as we scrambled to put ourselves back into check. All I could think of was, I was going to die, and my Dad wasn't the one who was going to kill me.

Jenn's Dad got that pleasure.

"Go back into the shower," Jenn whispered, ushering me in that direction. "While I go get dressed in my room."

"My clothes are still in your room," I said, turning around to get them.

"I'll bring them to you in a minute," she said. "Keep your trunks on, okay?"

"Yes," I said, climbing back into the shower we had left running.

Not a moment to soon either.

"Jenn?" called out Mr. Tate, as he walked into the house.

"Be out in a minute," Jenn called, from her room.

"Who's in the shower?" I heard him ask.

"Ryc," she replied, obviously stepping out of her room. "We went swimming down at the river, and I let him borrow a pair of your trunks. It was okay, wasn't it?"

"Yes," he said. "But why is he in the shower?"

"We took turns washing the sand off," Jenn stated. "He still has your trunks on."

"That's interesting," Mr. Tate laughed. "Why on earth would he take a shower wearing swimming trunks?"

"He didn't want to get caught naked in the house," Jenn replied, and they both busted out laughing.

I just laid my head against the shower wall, and thanked God we hadn't got caught doing something else. I would have been locked away for life, with the keys melted down to something else. My asking Dad to trust me, would have all been in vain, and rubbed in my face to the point where I wore it on my forehead. It would have been like the mark of Cain.

That is, if he didn't kill me first.

I won't deny that the experience wasn't something special, because it was. I would have to be a fool to think any less. I mean, was it all that wrong of a thing for us to do? I guess in some ways it was, and in some ways it wasn't. Yes, because we were tempting waters we had no business in just yet, and no, because you should experience that kind of thing with someone you loved. That was what we were doing, in the gentle spray of the shower.

The responsibility that comes with testing those waters was something neither one of us was really ready for. One, because we were still in school. Two, we couldn't afford the out come of raising a child, with no job to support us, if she were to have gotten pregnant. The third reason, which goes with the second, is that it could cut short the path's we wanted to take in our lives. That was I finally realized was, what my Dad was getting at.

The only problem I could see now was would I be as wise the next time we found ourselves in those waters?

# CHAPTER TWENTY-SEVEN

"HEY, RYC?" CALLED DONNY Long, from his truck, as I parked my bike in front of the Floating Store.

What now? I asked myself, when I looked up to see who it was.

"I hear you've put together a band," he said, walking over to me.

"We're working on it," I replied, wondering how he knew.

"That's cool," he said, with a smile. The kind of smile I didn't really trust. "Do you think you'll be good enough to play a gig for me?"

"When?" I asked, not sure I really wanted to deal with him.

"A couple of weekends from now," he said. "My parents are going on a private vacation, and said that I could have an end of the summer party for my friends."

"We might be able to put together a couple of songs by then," I stated.

"Great," he smiled, even bigger than before. "I'll let you know the exact date and all, okay?"

"Sure," I said, as we shook hands on the deal.

"About your girlfriend," he said. "I'm sorry I got out of line with you on that."

"It's okay," I said, wondering what this was leading to.

"Great," he smiled. "Why don't you bring her a long?"

"She's in the band," I smiled.

"Cool," he said, and headed back to his truck.

If I knew Donny Long at all, I knew he was up to something other just having us play at his party. I figured that, because he has never liked me from the start, and I could say the same thing. Donny Long was a looser waiting to happen.

The only thing I could figure is, Debbi must have told him what I wanted her to, and he wanted to teach me a lesson. Either that, or he wanted to make another play for Jenn. Knowing that would be enough to provoke me into fighting. I didn't like either one of those thoughts. Mostly because I really didn't like to fight, and I wasn't sure of the damage I could do if I got mad.

Therefore, whatever he had planned, I would be watching for it. Like a hawk ready to take its prey. The surprise would be his down fall, in the very realm he set into motion. People like that, always deserved what they got, and I would make sure Donny got what was coming to him. Even if I lost myself.

"Ryc," Roy called, riding up beside me. "Tell me that wasn't Donny Long I saw you talking to."

"I wish I could," I said. "He found out about our band, and wants us to play a gig."

"When?" Roy asked, with a look of shock on his face.

"In a couple of weeks," I replied. "Do you think we can get a few songs down by then?"

"Maybe," Roy said. "I just wouldn't trust Donny Long any further than I could drool."

"You either, huh?" I said.

I quickly told Roy about the run in Jenn and I had with Donny, and what Debbi and I had cooked up. He agreed that there was probably something else cooking on the back burner of Donny's head, and promised to help keep an eye on things at the party.

Usually, when two different people feel that something isn't quite right, they're usually right about the feeling. I took the information to heart, and prepared myself for the worse possible answer. What else could I do? If I've learned anything about guys like Donny, it was to beware of their actions.

Since Jenn may very well be the thing he was after, I would have to stand my ground. Which was probably something else my Dad would find to bitch about. Especially, if he knew there was a girl involved.

Something told me I couldn't win, even if I did.

## CHAPTER TWENTY-EIGHT

JENN WAS THRILLED TO death, when she heard the news about our first gig. Even though she held her own reservations about whom we were playing for. The same reservations that Roy and I held. When you have, or start a bad reputation, it just seems to follow you around forever. Donny's mouth is living proof of it.

We decided to practice on Jenn's deck, because it was the closest thing we could find that looked anything like a stage. Not to mention that it would be a real hassle trying to move Jenn's drum set back and forth, every time we wanted to practice.

"Can you really play those drums?" Roy asked, as we were setting up. "I mean, I've never really seen a girl that could play drums, in a rock band."

Jenn just smiled, sat behind her drums, and started playing an out of this world drum solo. Roy looked at me, I looked at Roy, and then we both looked at Jenn, and finally back at each other.

"Guess that answers your question," I said, when she wrapped it up.

"Shut up," Roy laughed, hitting a few cords on his bass. "Let's play some rock and roll."

We worked about three hours on the arrangements of several songs, figuring we would probably do at least two sets of three songs, before calling it a night. It was a party, you know. A party full of wild and crazy teen-agers.

Mr. Tate pulled into the driveway, unaware to us, and listened to our last song of the day. All of which I had written myself. We decided that if we were going to be an original band, we were going to play only original songs.

"Here we are locked in sweet embrace
With you kissing my face
Knowing how much I love you
And feeling it true
But what I've got to ask
Ain't that easy of a task
Oh, but it's true
I need an answer from you
Is it over yet?
Have you walked away?
Is it over yet?
This thing I pray
Is it over yet?
I've wanted and waited forever
For us to be together
And I know you have to
With every I love you
Life has kept us a part
Except true here in the heart
What I've got to ask
Ain't that great a task?
Is it over yet?
Have you walked away?
Is it over yet?
This thing I pray
Is it over yet?"

"That was great," Mr. Tate said, clapping his hands, as he walked up behind us.

"Hi, Dad," Jenn said, when she saw him.

Roy and I chimed in our hello at the same time.

"Was that one of your songs, Ryc?" Mr. Tate asked, looking at my notebook full of songs.

"Yes, Sir," I replied, with a smile.

"You're very talented," he said.

"You really liked the way we sounded?" I asked.

"I'm honestly amazed at what I heard coming from the three of you," he smiled. "I'm not saying that just to swell your heads. It's an honest statement."

"How good is that, Mr. Tate?" Roy asked.

"If you keep playing the way I heard you play," he replied. "In a few years, I'll sign you to the label I work for."

"All right!" the three of us all yelled at once.

"What do you call your band?"

"We don't really have a name yet," I stated. "But we're working on it. We decided to get our sound down first."

"Good idea," Mr. Tate smiled.

"How about 'Two Guys and a Girl?" Jenn offered.

"It works for me," Roy added.

"Two Guys and a Girl' it is," I said, and hit a cord on my guitar.

"I think you guys had better pack it in for the night," Mr. Tate said, pointing up toward the sky. "It looks like we're gonna get wet."

He was right. No sooner had we got the equipment into the house, did the heavens open up wide, with a raging storm. Mr. Tate took Roy and I home in his car, because it was raining too hard for us to ride our bikes.

"Wanna go for the ride?" Mr. Tate asked, Jenn.

"No," she said. "I'm not feeling too well. I think I'm gonna lie down for a while."

"I'll be right back, boys," Mr. Tate said, and walked into the house with Jenn.

"See you guys later," Jenn called, over her shoulder.

"Is she, okay?" Roy asked. "I noticed she was looking kind of pale earlier."

"I hope so," I said, with what must have been a look of concern on my face. "She's been doing that a lot lately."

"Doing what?" Roy asked.

"Getting sick," I replied.

Deep down inside, I was worried about her. First the nose bleeds, then the needing to rest, and now this. Maybe it was just me, but something sure wasn't right. Maybe it was me over reacting, because I didn't want to see her feeling sick, or anything. Then again, something about it still didn't add up.

Like a lot of things these days.

Jenn never talked about our little fantasy trip in the shower, and I figured it was just as well. Only I couldn't just stop thinking about it the way she seemed to. It was one of the most romantic moments we had ever shared, and it really bothered me that it seemed like it never really happened.

Then again, the two of us haven't been alone long enough to talk about it, since it happened. Maybe that was it. Maybe I was just over reacting again.

I was thankful Jenn had decided to stay home, because my Dad was standing on the front porch, when Mr. Tate dropped me off. If he had seen Jenn, she would have more than likely kissed me good-bye (which she didn't, by the way), and my Dad would have gone off his rocker, once he got his hands on me.

That was a scene I didn't want them to see. I was going to have a hard enough time getting him to let me go to this party. Knowing him, he would figure that there was more to it, than just me playing with my band. "Rock and roll only brings out the bad side of kids," I could hear him saying. "There won't be just a band playing. There'll be sex, pot, and booze."

I was hoping, really hoping, that if he knew how much I believed in my music, and that this was really my first gig, he'd let me go. That was provided nothing came a long to get in the way of my hopes. As you well know, my Dad was the kind of character that probably wouldn't give in that easy.

I think I've said this before. He had his own set of rules. "It's either my way, or my way." He had this habit of reminding us of that rule, every time we did something he didn't like.

Yet, he did give me a break with Carol Anne. Maybe that would be considered a good sign. A sign that things were changing, and he really was trying to understand me.

I hope so.

# CHAPTER TWENTY-NINE

I FELL A SLEEP that night, listening to the rain, and thinking about my experience in the shower with Jenn. I wondered about how far we would have gone, if her father hadn't come home, and how magical it might have been. I wondered about why we hadn't talked about it since the day it happened.

That was probably put off, by what I said earlier. We hadn't really been left alone since then. Either we weren't together, her farther was there, or we were practicing for our gig at Donny Long's. Yet, I knew the thoughts had to be there for both of us. I could kind of see it in her eyes. Every time she looked at me. I can't really explain it to you. I guess, it was more of a feeling, then anything. Maybe it was just me.

What else was I supposed to do? I'd never really been that far with a girl before, and was completely surprised at how natural it all was.

I was really new at this funny little thing called love. So new in fact, I found myself thinking about the things my Dad kept telling me. I knew in some weird way, he was trying to protect me from myself, and that was kind of cool. Yet, at the same time, I knew that the temptations to go beyond the limits I had set for myself were far greater than anything I had ever known.

Was that really love, or was it just being a teen-ager?

God, this was getting harder and harder to understand. They shouldn't have called us teen-agers. They should have called us confused instead. Why? Because that's exactly what we were. Confused. On one hand, it was wrong to tempt that kind of water, and on the other hand, we were going to learn them sooner or later.

A gentle tapping awaked me on my bedroom window. At first I thought it was just the rain, but quickly figured out that someone was there. When I looked to see who it was, I saw a dripping wet Carol Anne looking back at me.

"Carol Anne?" I whispered, opening the window. "What are you doing here?"

"Thinking," she slurred.

"Don't you mean drinking?" I asked, with a smile.

"That's what I said," she smiled, and stumbled forward into the side of the house.

"Are you drunk?" I asked, knowing that she was several sheets into the wind, and not really looking for away back just yet.

"A little," she smiled. "Okay, maybe more than a lot."

"Are you crazy?" I asked, not really believing she could do something as stupid as get drunk.

"Which am I?" she asked. "Drunk or crazy?"

"Both," I said, with a little laugh. "What do you want?"

"Can I stay with you tonight?" she asked, with a set of pleading puppy dog eyes. "My Dad will kill me if I come home like this."

"My Dad will kill me," I reminded her. "If he finds you here."

"Please?" she asked, still wearing those puppy dog eyes, and suddenly slid down the side of the house.

"Carol Anne?" I called, sticking my head out the window.

"Here," she said, sticking one of her hands in the air.

"Let me put my jeans on," I said, as she crawled back up the side of the house, and hung in the window.

"Why?" she asked. "I've seen you naked."

"C'mon," I said, and went to help her through the window instead. "Just keep it down, before you wake someone else up."

"Okay," she whispered, and crashed to the floor.

That's when I heard the door to my parent's room open, and footsteps fall toward my room.

"Don't move," I whispered to Carol Anne, as the door to my room opened.

"Ryc?" Mom's voice called out into the darkness, and turned on the light. "Are you all right?"

"Yeah," I whispered. "I fell a sleep, with my guitar on the bed, and knocked it off onto the floor."

"Okay," she said, backing out the door, and reaching for the light switch.

"I'll get that," I said. "I need to see to put my guitar on its stand."

"Okay," she said, shutting the door. "Go back to sleep when you're finished."

"I will," I said.

"Goodnight," she called, and went back into her room.

"Goodnight, Mom," I called in a low voice, but knew she couldn't hear me.

Man, that was close.

"Carol Anne?" I whispered, bending down to where she lay on the floor.

"Here," she said, setting up against the bed.

"You're not going to get sick, are you?"

"No," she laughed. "I already did that."

"What am I gonna do with you?" I asked, brushing back her wet hair, out of her face.

"Take care of me," she replied, with those same puppy dog eyes.

"Okay," I said, lifting her up off the floor. "You've got to sneak out of here, come first light, and go home."

"I will," she said, hugging me. "Can I borrow a shirt?"

"Sure," I said, as she pulled her wet jeans off, and hung them over my desk chair.

"I don't really want to get you into any trouble with your Dad," she said, and pulled off her wet T-shirt.

"You won't," I whispered, turning around to face her. "If you stop talk. . ."

I was caught off guard, by the sight of her standing there in her panties. I'd forgotten she didn't like to wear bras in the summer time.

"Something wrong?" she asked, not bothering to cover herself.

"No," I kind of choked, and handed her the shirt.

She just smiled, rolled her eyes into the back of her head, and went out like a light. There was nothing I could really do, but let her sleep it off.

"Oh, God," I said, as an after thought, and hung the shirt back up.

I pulled her up in the bed, to lay her head on one of the pillows, and to cover her up. With that done, I crawled into bed beside her, and decided to try and stay awake the rest of the night. She rolled over, put her body up next to mine, and draped her arm across my chest. She felt cold and damp, as I brushed her hair out of her face again.

What was going through her head? I wondered, as her sleep became heavier and heavier. Was this how she dealt with the confusion we were all going through? Was this her answer to deal with not having the love she felt for me? I had know way of knowing what the answer was, or even if I ever would.

"What am I going to do with you?" I whispered, and kissed her lightly on the head.

Sleep was slowly starting to take its toll on me as well. I knew if anyone found out she was there, hell would be the price I paid for it. What else could I have done? She was my best friend, and I cared about her. It wasn't like I was thinking of anything else, if you know what I mean? She was in trouble, and I had to be there for her. That was my job. That's what best friends do for each other. I couldn't let her go home to face whatever it was she was afraid to go home to.

She would have done it for me. That's the way we were with each other. There was no other avenue that I could see to take.

I decided that if by chance we were to get caught in bed together, I would just tell the truth. Right. My Dad would still fly off the handle, my Mom would have a heart attack, her Dad would shoot both of us, and Jenn would breakup with me. No one would ever understand the truth. They would just pass it off, as us being two horny teen-agers, who got caught in bed together, with their clothes off.

I had to stay awake.

As sleep took me away to my dreams, I kept telling myself, I had to stay awake. I just had to, no matter what. There was a lot riding on me doing just that. I just had to.

No such luck.

## CHAPTER THIRTY

"RYC?" I HEARD MY name whispered, as if it were far away.

"What?" I asked.

"Wake up, Ryc," I heard Carol Anne's voice whisper this time, and sat straight up in the bed.

I couldn't believe I had fallen a sleep.

"Carol Anne?" I asked, looking straight at her.

"Where are my clothes?" she asked, setting up in the bed, holding the blankets around her upper half.

"On the chair where you left them," I answered.

"How did I get here?" she asked, frozen where she sat.

"You don't remember?" I asked, and laid back down on the bed.

"No," she said, with this really frightened look. "We didn't. . . well, you know?"

I smiled.

"Ryc?" she asked, and I knew it was time for me to get even with her.

"Yeah," I replied, deciding that maybe I would just tease her a little. "We went all the way, and man was it great."

"Oh, my God," she said, and laid back down beside me. "I didn't know this was gonna happen."

"It surprised me too," I said, starting to find it hard not to laugh.

"What are we gonna do?" she asked, staring at the ceiling.

"I don't know," I said, watching her face.

"What if I get pregnant?" she asked, and looked at me.

"Relax," I said, leaning up on my right elbow. "We didn't do anything that would get either of us into trouble."

"I knew it," she smiled, and leaned up on her left elbow. "What did we do?"

"Nothing," I replied.

"Are you sure?" she asked, and looked under the blanket at herself. "If you haven't noticed, I am over half naked."

"You passed out," I confessed. "And I fell a sleep, watching over you."

"Why are my clothes off?" she asked, lifting the blanket again, as if to make sure she was the way she thought she was.

"You came here last night, drunk as a dog," I replied. "And asked if you could stay all night."

"That doesn't explain what happened to my clothes," she stated.

"Your clothes were soaking wet," I said. "You asked to borrow a shirt, took off your clothes, and passed out before I could give you the shirt."

"We can't let anyone find out about this," she said. "No one will believe that it's an innocent act shared between two friends."

"That's why you need to get dressed," I smiled. "And sneak home before anyone misses you."

"They won't," she said. "They think I stayed all night with one of my girlfriends."

"That's not gonna work here," I smiled. "My Dad won't see me as one of your girlfriends."

"Yeah," she said, and sat back up in the bed. "Could you look the other way for a moment?"

"Why?" I smiled, teasing her again. "I've already seen you naked."

"That maybe so, Mr. Lewis," she replied. "Right now, I feel just a little bit stupid. If you know what I mean?"

"Kinda how I felt last night," I said, covering my head.

"Thanks," she said, and a moment later. "You can uncover now."

"No problem," I said, as she started out the window.

"I'll call you later, okay?"

"Sure," I said.

"I love you," she said, crawling back through the window, and kissed me.

"I love you too," I said, as she crawled back out the window into the rain.

"Bye," she said.

"Bye," I said, as she took off down the road.

So far, so good. I pulled the blankcts back up around me, and tried to go back to sleep. My mind was racing with the memory of what had taken place, and how neither one of us really took advantage of it. Carol Anne was on her way home; as if she had walked home in the rain from her girlfriends, and no one would ever expect there was another truth to it. No one that is, but Carol Anne and me.

I couldn't have been more wrong.

# CHAPTER THIRTY-ONE

I was sitting on the front porch, when Dad got home. It was the same day Carol Anne had made her escape from my bedroom. I could tell by the way he stayed in the car, staring at me, that something was wrong.

How could he have known?

"Come into the kitchen," He said, as he walked into the house. "Your mother and I want to talk to you."

"Okay," I said, and followed him inside.

I wasn't sure if he knew, or not. I just knew that something wasn't quite right, and that it somehow involved me. That usually meant that it was something I didn't really want to know. Lately, when my Dad was mad, no one wanted to know what it was.

"What's the problem?" I asked, stepping into the kitchen.

"Who the hell do you think you are?" he screamed into my face, and slammed me back against the wall.

"What do you mean?" I asked, knowing full well that he somehow found out about Carol Anne and me sleeping together in the same bed.

"You had that girl in bed with you last night," he snapped.

"I can explain," I said, as he grabbed me by the hair, and drug me into the living room.

"Jim!" Mom cried.

"Stay out of this, Jane," Dad yelled, and threw me back into the hall.

"Listen to what he has to say," Mom said, crying, as she stepped away from me.

"Stay out of it," Dad spit, and shoved her to the floor.

"Don't treat her like that," I yelled, climbing back to my feet.

"Or what?" he asked, and backhanded me in the mouth.

"Jim!" Mom screamed again.

I just stood there, staring at him. It was obvious. He had been drinking. That's the way he acted, when he got drunk. Like an out of control idiot, taking his rage out on those weaker than he was, or on whoever got into his way.

"Now, explain to me why you had a half naked girl in bed with you last night," he demanded, and back me up against the wall again.

"It's not what you think," I said, with my own rage building up inside of me.

Smack! He hit me, and busted my lower lip.

"Now," he demanded again. "Explain it to me."

"Why?" I asked. "So you can hit me again."

"You're pushing it, Ryc," he warned, with sheer terror in his eyes.

"I thought I made a good judgment call," I said.

"A judgment call?" he repeated, and jerked me up off the floor.

"Go ahead, Dad," I said, spitting blood. "Hit me again. That's what you're good at."

He threw me up against the wall, and walked into the living room. Mom came over to check on me, but I pushed her away. I didn't want her to get hurt any more than she already was. She had been pushed around enough because of me, and I wasn't going to let it happen anymore. Especially, in case he wasn't finished hitting me.

"Where did I go wrong?" he asked, more to himself than us.

"By getting drunk," I replied.

"Don't get smart with me," he stated, turning around to face me.

"You asked," I said, knowing full well that I would probably only make things worse.

"You asked me to trust you with that girl," he stated, coming up in to my face again. "Did you not?"

"Yeah," I said, wondering where this was leading to. "I did ask."

"Then could you tell me why I found her half naked in bed with you this morning?" he asked, without taking a breath.

"It's a long story," I said, and leaned back up against the wall on my own.

"Why don't you tell it to me?" he said, walking into the kitchen, where he sat down at the table, and waited for me to do the same.

I told him the complete story, to the best of my knowledge, as to how Carol Anne ended up in my bed, and didn't leave out a single detail. He listened to me, but I wasn't sure he was really hearing me. He had this disbelieving look on his face that suggested he wasn't really buying it. To be honest with you, I know it must have been a hard sell.

"What else could I do?" I asked, when I finished my side of it.

"You honestly expect me to buy that, don't you?" he asked, looking at me, with an unknown grin. I say unknown, because I had never seen it on him before.

"It's the truth, Dad," I said. "She's my best friend, and it's my job to protect her from harm. I wouldn't have been doing that, if I hadn't taken her in."

"Kids today," he said, and looked at my mother. "What do you make of all this?"

"I don't like it," Mom said, and looked over at me. "But I believe he's telling us the truth."

"You would," Dad said. "It's just that I can't see a teenage boy and girl being that close, without anything going on."

"Call Carol Anne," I suggested. "Ask her to come over for a few minutes. If I tell her that I told you the truth, she wouldn't lie about it."

"Dial the number," Dad said. "I would like to get to the bottom of this."

I picked up the phone, dialed the number, and handed the phone to my Dad. I figured that if I were ever going to get anywhere with him, I needed to level with him, and let him do the talking. So far, he wasn't jumping the gun the way he did when he first got home, and was now at least trying to understand what I was telling him.

"May I speak to Carol Anne?" he asked. "Yes, this is Ryc Lewis' father."

"Is she there?" I asked, but he only motioned me to wait.

"Carol Anne?" he asked. "Hi, this is Ryc's Dad. Could you come over here for a few minutes, and help clear up something? Thank you. We'll be waiting."

He hung up the phone, and said that she would be here just as fast as she could. I knew that she would be really nervous about the call, and that she would more than likely figure out what it was all about. I also knew that if she knew that I had confessed what I knew about it, she would do the same thing if confronted with the issue.

That's why we were best friends. Despite the other problems we had at the moment, we would always be true to each other as friends go.

I had that much faith in her, and wasn't about to doubt it now.

I knew her that well.

# CHAPTER THIRTY-TWO

CAROL ANNE SHOWED UP a few minutes later, standing in our front door, with this really scared look on her face. Her eyes told me that her worse fears had come true. In her shoes, and not knowing my Dad all that well, I would be scared too.

"My Dad saw us in bed together this morning," I said. "I told him the truth as to how you got there."

"Okay," she said.

"I'll make this fast," Dad said, staring at her. "Were you drunk?"

"Yes, Sir," she replied.

"Was Ryc drunk?" he asked, sitting down on the arm of the sofa.

"No, Sir," she replied, keeping her eyes on my Dad's. "He wasn't even with me."

"Where did you get what you drank?" Mom asked.

"I took it from my Dad's stuff," she said.

"Why?" Dad asked.

"For personal reasons," she replied. "Reasons that don't concern why Ryc's in trouble."

"I disagree with you, Carol Anne," Dad stated. "Those reasons are why you ended up with Ryc, aren't they?"

"Kind of," Carol Anne replied.

"Okay," Dad said, sliding into the sofa seat, but not sitting back. "Let me put it this way. Why did you go to Ryc's bedroom window?"

"He's my friend," she said, and started to cry. "He's the only real friend I have. Look, Mr. and Mrs. Lewis, nothing sexual happened between us last night. Ryc is one of the nicest guys a girl could know. You should be proud to have a son like him."

"I am," Dad said, getting up to go over to where she stood. "Like all parents, I just had to be sure of the truth."

"I didn't want to get anyone in trouble," she cried. "I just didn't have anywhere else to go."

"It's okay," Dad said, pulling her to him. Which really wasn't like the Dad I knew. "Tell you what. We'll keep this among the four of us."

"Okay," Carol Anne replied.

"That's provided it doesn't happen again," added Dad.

"It won't," she said.

"It goes the same for me," I said.

"If you have a problem you need an adult to talk to," Dad said. "You can talk to one of us."

"Thanks," she said. "I'll try to remember that."

"Okay, Ryc," Dad said. "If you'll walk your friend home, we'll talk about this some more later."

"Sure," I said, and led Carol Anne outside.

"Thank you, Mr. and Mrs. Lewis," Carol Anne said, looking back over her shoulder, as we walked out the door.

"That wasn't like my Dad at all," I said, once we got out of ear shot.

"I thought he handled it rather nicely," she smiled.

"That's the problem," I said. "Normally, I would still be pulling my face from out of the wall."

"Looks like you already did that," Carol Anne said, and touched my busted lip. "Does it hurt very much?"

"A little," I said, pulling back from her touch.

"What stopped him from hitting you anymore?"

"I guess it was because I started standing my ground," I said, because I really didn't know the answer.

"Maybe he's trying to understand you," she said. "You know, like fathers' are supposed to do."

"I hope so," I smiled, still worried that there was something else brewing behind the way he was acting. It just wasn't right for him to act that way.

"Do you think he saw my boobs?" Carol Anne asked.

"Yes," I smiled. "I think maybe he did."

"Oh, God," she said. "This is really embarrassing."

"Why?" I asked, tugging at her blouse in a teasing manner. "I think your boobs look kind of nice."

"Yeah," she smiled, pushing my hand away. "But what would Jenn think?"

"That's another story," I said. "One I would much rather not have to defend."

"I hear ya," Carol Anne said, and kissed me on the cheek. "It's our secret, okay."

"Thanks," I said, and kissed her back on the cheek.

"For what?" she asked.

"For being who you are," I said, and started walking away.

"You to," she said, and watched me until I was over the hill that separated our two homes.

As I walked the rest of the way home, I kept wondering about what my Dad was up to, and why he suddenly changed in mid stroke? It just wasn't like the characteristics I was used to, when he got bent out of shape. Oh, God, I suddenly thought. I'm starting to act like my father in away. We were trading places, and I was going overboard with the way I was thinking. Just like he did, when he thought about me.

I wanted to scream.

Okay, okay, I'll give him a break. Maybe I was over reacting. Maybe he was trying to understand me? Maybe he was starting to believe that all those times he had jumped my case about girls was starting to rub off on me? Maybe he was giving me a break?

I sure hoped so.

I'd hated to wake up one morning, and find out I wasn't here any-more, because I had pissed him off. That wouldn't be good at all.

Maybe we were both learning something from all of this? Maybe it was time that we both opened our eyes to our differences, and started acting like real people? I mean we can't stay at war with each other forever, can we? What do you gain from something like that? There's got to be a middle ground somewhere.

It still made me want to scream.

## CHAPTER THIRTY-THREE

THE NEXT DAY, I was in Jenn's living room, waiting for her to get dressed. As I waited, I noticed a picture on the mantel of her and an older woman. They were wearing happy smiles, and appeared to be having a good time. The woman must have been her mother, because Jenn looked several years younger, and the woman favored her a lot.

"Those were happy times," Jenn said, coming up behind me. "It was just before Mom got really sick."

"You both look happy," I stated, looking at the picture. "She was a very beautiful lady."

"That she was," Jenn smiled, taking the picture from me, and sitting it back upon the mantel. "Sometimes, I really miss her."

"I'm not sure how I would take losin' my Mom," I said. "I imagine that it would totally floor me."

"It takes a long time to get back up from," Jenn said, with a single tear running down her cheek. "It gets easier, as time goes by. Sometimes for a brief moment, now and then, you can find yourself climbing back up from where you've just been."

"I can tell that you really loved her a lot," I said, and wiped away the tear with my fingers. I know it didn't erase the pain, but it did show that I felt for her.

"Thanks," she said, holding my hand to the side of her face.

We never talked about it after that. I figured she didn't need any more reminders of the loss, and I really didn't want to see her cry anymore. Life was hard enough as it was, with all its set backs, and all the tears that find there way to our eyes for one reason or another. Like so many of the things we fought with our many temptations, tears weren't one of the things we needed.

I don't really know, because she never said, but I kind of figured she respected my not pushing the issue of her mother. I would have liked to have known, but figured I could wait until it came on its own accord.

I loved her that much.

Like I said, we never talked about it again. I did, however, kind of write about it in one of my songs sometime later. It was my way of dealing with a touchy subject. With words I never said, and words I never showed her. Words I never really showed anyone, because that's the way I was. I had my place, and my private moments that were mind alone.

My lyric portfolio is filled with such thoughts and feelings. One day, they would hopefully be the makings of a great songwriter. Someday, somewhere in time, beyond these moments when the words hurt so much.

Maybe to a time when the moment became a thing of the past, and we could look back on it with a fragile smile that whispered its thank you. One that said it's okay. I'm better now because of who and what you are. It's funny, but that was who I was. The lonely runner, who took on the weight of the world, and never said a word. Because the world wasn't always as forgiving as I was. Not by any measure. . .

> "In the back of my mind
> I can see so well
> All the yesterdays behind
> The path leading out of hell
> And all the tears that show
> Force me to find a smile

That I didn't know
In my deepest moment of denial
Now I'm up to my ears
In those sentimental tears
Trying to overcome
The urge to run
With all my silent fears
In those sentimental tears
Dancing in the back of my head
I try to remember the words said
That was not to be
Something I could see
When the damage was done
We were falling into the sun
And the silent message read
That she was already dead
Now I'm up to my ears
In those sentimental tears
In days gone by
When I could not cry
Without all the fears
In those sentimental tears."

## CHAPTER THIRTY-FOUR

"SING ME A LOVE song, Ryc," Jenn asked, one afternoon when I was over, and she was feeling under the weather.

"Sure," I smiled, because I'd really do anything for her.

"Make it one that I'm gonna remember for the rest of my life," she said, adjusting herself on the sofa to listen to me.

"Does it have to be one of mine?" I asked, sitting down at the piano.

"No," she smiled. "But why would you want to sing someone else's material?"

"Because the song I have in mind is the most beautiful love song I've heard," I replied. "I think it best says the kinda thing I'd like to be able to say, and it's also an Elvis song."

"Elvis?" she questioned, with a sparkle in her eyes, and another smile on her lips. "Can I ask which one?"

"Anyway You Want Me," I replied, and started playing. "Would you like me to do it like Elvis, or like me?"

"Surprise me," she said, and laid her head back into the sofa.

"I'll do it like Elvis," I said. "Because it's his song, and only Elvis could ever do this one right."

She sat there with all eyes watching me as I went through the motions of singing to her my favorite Elvis song. I could tell that she was deeply moved by my performance, but I could tell that she wasn't at all feeling well. That made me wonder if I should even be there or not, but then again where else would I be?

Near the end of the song she put both her hands to her mouth, and whispered, "I love you" to me. In all the times I've ever preformed Elvis that was the one time I think I felt the most like he must have been.

"How was that, Baby?" I asked, in perfect Elvis voice.

"It was beautiful," she whispered. "What do you think, Daddy?"

I didn't know he had come into the room.

"Let's just say that I think Elvis might be worried about his throne if he had a chance to hear you," he said, with a smile.

"No way," I said, feeling a little embarrassed.

"Yes way," he said, coming a little further into the room. "It was a haunting performance that I think will one day take you far."

"Thanks," I said.

"You kids go on with what you were doing," he said. "I still have a lot of work to catch up on."

"Sorry we disturbed you, Daddy," stated Jenn, as he was walking back down the hall.

"No problem," he said, over his shoulder. "I enjoyed the break."

"Thanks again, Mr. Tate," I called out, as he entered his office.

"Thank you," he called back.

"Man," I said, to Jenn. "That scared the hell out of me."

"You don't want to know what it did to me," she smiled, laying back down on the sofa.

"Sure, I do," I said, going back over to sit next to her on the floor.

"Let me answer that by asking you another question," she said, looking me dead serious in the eyes.

"Okay," I said, wondering where this was going.

"Do you ever think about what might have happened that day in the shower if my Dad hadn't come home when he did?" she asked, and I knew full well what she was thinking about.

"Yeah, I do," I said.

"You're that good," she smiled. "Now give us a kiss before the moment gets away from us."

"Maybe I should do Elvis more often," I whispered, with my lips pressing into hers.

"Maybe you should," she said, and bit me.

I'm not going to go into any detail on the subject, but the truth is I've had several erotic dreams on the subject of Jenn and I in the shower. I'd be a complete and total liar if I tried to tell you I didn't think about it.

The only bad part about those kind of dreams and thoughts was that something always seemed to happen to never let me see how they played out. Maybe it was all that stuff my Dad fed me about sex, and it being my baby if I got myself into trouble. I'd like to think that it was more something I had decided for myself rather than something someone tried to program into me.

Whatever the reason was, it was mine, right?

We are all responsible for or own actions and thoughts and dreams. Even if others can influence the hell out of them.

What I knew was that I loved Jenn, and I had plenty of time for the adventure that lie ahead of us.

Right?

# CHAPTER THIRTY-FIVE

I WAS IN THE bathroom the next morning, looking at my face in the mirror, when Dad happened to walk by, and catch me. He didn't say anything right off, but I could tell he was waiting for the right moment to do just that.

"What are you looking at?" he asked, totally out of character for him. He's been like that a lot lately, and I didn't get it.

"Nothing really," I replied, and looked at my chin. "I was just wondering how long it would take me to grow sideburns like Elvis?"

"You have to start shaving," he said, stepping into the bathroom beside me. "Shave the area you want to grow, let it grow out a little more each time you shave it, and eventually you'll have your sideburns."

"I don't have a razor," I said.

"It'll happen soon enough," he smiled, and went on about whatever it was he was doing.

That night, when I got home, and ready to take a shower. There was a razor, blades, and shaving cream sitting on my bed. It touched me that Dad had taken the time to do that, without making a big deal out of it. In many ways, I figure he was fighting the notion that I was growing up, and was trying to give me the space to do so.

"It's okay, Dad," I said, to myself. "Sometimes it's hard for me to see what's beyond the what already is stage."

I know, I know, we can't always see the forest, for the trees.

"Do you want me to show you how it's done?" He asked, catching me in the bathroom, with his gift.

"Sure," I smiled, and handed him the razor.

First he showed me how to put the shaving cream on, as if anyone could have done that little trick. Then he showed me how to shave the area I wanted to shave. That was a bit harder, and a bit scarier. Amazing enough, he was very gentle about the way he handled the razor, when he was gliding it across my face.

"If you just want sideburns," he said, handing me back the razor. "I would just shave that area for now. Otherwise, you'll have a full beard, and I don't think you're ready for that."

"Probably not," I replied, with a laugh, and splashes of shaving cream still on my face.

Like I said before, Dad wasn't all that bad. We've had our good moments too. The only thing about it is, I wish there had been a lot more good moments, than bad. The saddest part of all is we don't always get what we want.

Those are the stupid moments we waste in conflict, over one thing or another. Things that don't really matter, and make you look the way they are. Stupid. Life is too damn short to waste on issues that don't need to be brought to war. It's even sadder knowing that it takes those kind of wars to open our eyes.

Only the moments before that realization, are lost forever, and can never be recaptured. Not for one instant, or one moment. Once it's gone, it's gone forever, and we are the stupid fools that lost it to a conflict that didn't need to be. . .

> "Daddy, I'm so afraid
> Of the mistakes I've made
> That I cannot see
> The way back to me
> Momma, why so many tears
> Your heart has cried in fears

That you couldn't see
It didn't have to be
But your baby, has become a man
On a road too nowhere
Where he seldom sees
No road left behind him
That tomorrow is way to far
To try to reach the shadowed soul
That has become a man
And he don't know why
Used to be wild and free
No chains that could bind
While cradled in the shores
Of my youthful heart
When I had to run
Grow up with the pack
That allowed me to be
The only lonely one
Because your baby, has become a man
And he still don't know why."

# CHAPTER THIRTY-SIX

"I CAN'T BELIEVE YOUR Dad let you off so easy," Roy said, as he, myself, and Carol Anne walked down to the Floating Store.

"Me either," I stated. "It was like he was someone else."

"I can't believe he saw me topless," Carol Anne said, with an embarrassed smile.

"I can't believe you guys were in bed that way," Roy smirked. "And didn't do anything."

"Shut up," Carol Anne and I said, at the same time.

"Sorry," Roy said. "But you've got to admit that it's strange."

"Shut up," we said again.

It was all in good nature. Carol Anne and I both knew that Roy wasn't meaning any real harm by his statements. He was a good-natured boy that liked to razz you to the limit, if he had something like that on you, and thought he could get away with it.

"Hey, guys," Jenn called, from down the road.

"We'd better not say anything about this around Jenn," Carol Anne said, looking directly at Roy.

"Yeah," I agreed. "Jenn might not be so forgiving if she knew that her boyfriend had been sleeping in the same bed as her best friend."

"C'mon, guys," Roy said. "I'm not that heartless."

"No, you're not," Carol Anne replied. "It's just that if you're not warned, you might let it slip."

"I'm cool," Roy smiled.

"What's up?" Jenn asked, catching up to where we were waiting for her.

"We were getting a soda," I replied, as she wrapped her arms around me.

"Mind if I joined you?" she asked.

"That's why we waited for you," I smiled.

"Yeah," Roy said. "We were hoping that you would."

"Hey, Carol Anne," Jenn said, punching her lightly on the arm.

"Hey, Jenn," Carol Anne replied.

"Are you going to be able to see us play at Donny Long's?" Jenn asked. "It's gonna be a blast."

"I bet it is," Carol Anne said. "Only I can't make it. I have to go to Memphis with my Dad that weekend."

"We're going to record it," I said, and smiled at Carol Anne.

"You'll at least be able to hear us," Roy added.

"That'll be great," Carol Anne smiled.

"How about that coke?" Roy asked, changing the subject.

It was a good thing too. Even though we were all being cool about things, you could sense that something wasn't quite right. I really wasn't sure what it was, but I figured it had something to do with the way Carol Anne was coming across. Her actions seemed a bit frozen, now that Jenn was with us.

It could have all been in my head, because I had a lot of other stuff dancing around up there at the moment. Carol Anne's feelings. The band and our up coming gig. Sleeping in the same bed, and how it might look to others if they knew. Just so many things at once that I was glad Roy must have sensed something himself, to change the subject.

"Now that we have our cold drinks," Jenn said. "What do you suppose we all do now?"

"We need to practice," Roy suggested.

"You're right," I agreed.

143

"If you guys don't mind?" Carol Anne asked. "I think I'm gonna go on home for a while."

"Are you sure you don't want to come listen?" Jenn asked.

"Maybe next time," she replied, and slowly started up the road toward her house. "See ya later."

"See ya," we all chimed, as we watched her walk away.

"What's wrong with her?" Jenn asked.

"She's got a lot on her mind," I said.

"What kind of things?" Jenn asked.

"Her boyfriend lives in Memphis," I lied, knowing that there was no boyfriend in Memphis. "And she's stuck all the way out here in the nowhere land we call home."

"That's got to be hard," Jenn said.

"That's not to mention the fact that her two best friends don't seem to have as much time to spend with her as they once did," I reminded her.

"You're right," Jenn said, then stopped in her tracks. "Look, why don't we skip playing right now?"

"Why?" Roy asked.

"I think I need to go spend some time with a friend of ours," Jenn replied. "Is that okay with you two?"

"That's cool," Roy said.

"I'm okay with it," I said, and kissed her good-bye.

"Bye," she said, and took off after Carol Anne.

"I would hate to be in your shoes," Roy said, as we change direction, and headed toward my house.

"Why?" I asked.

"I'm not blind, Ryc," Roy stated. "I can see that both of those girls are in love with you."

"That obvious, huh?"

"Yeah," Roy said. "And the only one in the dark about it is your girlfriend."

"It isn't fair either," I said.

"Love never is," Roy smiled. "Besides, I thought you and Carol Anne had come to terms with this gig."

"So did I," I replied.

"C'mon, Lover boy," Roy said, and put me in a headlock. "This one's gonna be really hard to get out of."

He was right. It wasn't fair, and it was gonna be hard to get out of. I hated to be stuck in the middle. I hated it; because no matter what way I turned, someone was gonna get hurt.

The thing is, no one could see that someone was already hurt. In away, we were all hurt, and didn't know just how much. We were all innocent souls, who cared about each other so deeply; we would do anything to not be the one who did the hurting.

So why weren't we doing it?

Guess what? Being in the middle made me feel like the bad guy. I hated that feeling, because it's what wasn't fair about this.

It wasn't fair at all.

# CHAPTER THIRTY-SEVEN

I DON'T KNOW WHAT Jenn did, but she caught up with Roy and me riding our bikes, and told us that the practice was still on. Somehow, she'd got Carol Anne to come watch us play. I was both glad, and worried about it at the same time.

"We need someone our own age to give us an honest opinion about how we sound," Jenn said, as we all took our places on her deck. "Carol Anne has agreed to be our critic. Right, Carol Anne?"

"Yeah," smiled Carol Anne. "And you better be good."

"Are you going to write us up if we're not?" Roy asked.

"You bet," Carol Anne laughed, and we all joined in with her.

The mood was better than I had expected.

"Okay," I said. "Let's get this show on the road. Our critic awaits our introduction."

Roy showed off a little on his bass, as Jenn did a quick drum roll, and I followed with a mean guitar riff. When we were all finished, we stopped dead in our tracks, and looked over at Carol Anne. She had this disbelieving look on her face.

"You call that a band?" she asked.

"That's it," I said. "We've worked forever on getting it down."

"I should have gone home," she smiled.

"We call that little number, 'Putting You on the Spot," I said, with an ear-to-ear grin.

"Shut up," she smiled again. "And play me a real song."

"All right," I said, and started strumming one of my easier tunes, figuring it would be the best way to start. "Listen to the key I'm in, and then try to follow a long."

Roy and Jenn listened to the way I was playing, and then slowly started to join in. Once they figured out what I was doing, I prepared myself to come in with the lyrics. We decided we'd work the arrangements out as we went a long with each song we were gonna play.

"Yeah," I said, turning around to face them. "That's it. Feel the music. C'mon now, let's pick it up a little. One, two, three, let's rock."

We were all into it by then, playing as if we had been playing all our lives. The music had taken control, down a runaway track, moving us as a single unit with the power of its sweet embrace. We were rockin'.

> "Runnin' into the night
> Hidin' from the light
> To where you don't know
> But it haunts your very soul
> With a fear that can't be denied
> One you keep hidden inside
> Always giving just a little
> Not to get caught in the middle
> But enough to survive
> Dead or alive
> Runnin' into the night
> Hidin' from the light
> Afraid to let yourself be
> Alone and in love with me
> But love can't be denied
> If it's never been tried
> Just enough to survive
> Dead or alive
> I've let myself fall too deep
> For you not to keep

In touch with me
Cause we were meant to be
Runnin' into the night
Hidin' from the light
Just enough to survive
Dead or alive
Dead or alive."


"I think we've got it," I said, after we finished the song.

"It sounded really good," Roy smiled. "It was like we were professionals."

"Who'd believe it?" Jenn asked, with a double thumbs up sign.

"I'd just like to ask one thing," Carol Anne said, stopping all of us from our self-made glory.

We all looked at her, as if it were the end of the world. She was our critic, after all. We would have to value what she thought, and go from there.

"Do I get an autographed album?"

We all broke into laughter, and started throwing cups of water at her. I know stranger things have happened. But for us, three nobody kids from Tennessee, with no formal training, this was just about the best thing there was.

The music world was ours.

Okay, maybe it was our little corner of it.

It was enough.

# CHAPTER THIRTY-EIGHT

My Dad was so keen on the idea that I actually had a band; he even went down to Jenn's and hauled her drums and the rest of our equipment to Donny's for us. It was like he made a total turn around on the subject of me being a teen-ager.

"Who's the blonde?" He asked, as we were unloading the truck.

"She's the drummer," I replied, not sure how far I wanted to go with this new change.

"Does she have a name?" he asked, with a serious smile.

"Jennifer Tate," I said. "Her father promotes bands for a record company in Nashville."

"That's great," Dad said. "Is he gonna promote you?"

"He said we needed to stay with it for a couple of years." I replied. "We're good, but he thinks we'll be better if we stick with it a while."

"You know," he said. "I've never heard of a girl drummer before."

"Me neither," I smiled. "But I hear they're starting to emerge everywhere nowadays."

"She seems to have an eye out for you," he said, looking over my shoulder toward where she was standing.

"I'm the lead singer and guitar player," I smiled, hoping to change the subject.

"Why don't I know this girl?" he asked, turning his attention toward me.

"Do you want me to tell you the truth?" I asked. "Or come up with a really good lie?"

"The truth would be nice," he said, with a hurt frown.

"You were too busy worrying about what you thought I was doing," I replied, waiting for the explosion. "To take time to see what I was really doing."

"I'm sorry," he said, putting his hand on my shoulder. "I'm new at this having a teen-ager with a mind of his own. It's like you grew up over night, and somewhere a long the way I missed something."

"Dad?" I said, putting my hand on top of his. "I'm just as new at being a teen-ager, as you are at having one."

"Guess we both have a lot of learning to do," he smiled, and pulled his hand away.

"You know," I said. "I picked up the music from you."

"How did you pick it up from me?"

"Every time you would jump into a Hank Williams' song while we driving down the road," I confessed. "It inspired my imagination. I thought that it was so cool that I wanted to do it myself someday."

"I didn't know that," he said

"You never asked," I said, pulling out my electric guitar.

"Guess I was talking," he laughed. "When I should have been listening."

"Guess so," I smiled.

"Well," he said. "I'm gonna leave you to your party. Try to be home by midnight, okay?"

"Okay," I said.

"You are making a recording of this, aren't you?" he asked, as he started walking away.

"Yes, we are," I smiled even harder.

"Good," he said, continued on his way home.

He decided to leave the truck there, and pick it up with our instruments in the morning. He never said, but I think he really just wanted to walk home. He had a habit of taking long walks by himself, without letting anyone know where he was going.

I was kind of at a loss for words, as I watched him walking away. A part of me was trying to understand what was going on, while the other part was saying there has to be more to it. Which brings me back to that statement I made earlier, about needing to be called confused, rather than a teen-ager.

Sometimes, I just didn't get it.

"That was your Dad, huh?" Jenn asked, walking up beside me.

"That was him," I said.

"He sounds nice enough," Jenn stated. "When are you going to get the nerve to tell him about us?"

"When do you want me to?" I asked.

"Tomorrow," she smiled, kissed me, and walked into the house where we were setting up.

I really didn't know if it were such a great idea, or not. Considering the way, he was about the subject. Girls and rock and roll equaled sex in his book. That meant it wasn't going to be that easy a subject to deal with. Yet, at the same time, I knew it was something I couldn't keep to myself much longer.

Who knows? With the way he was acting now, he'd probably dance for joy.

Parents today. Who really understands them? One minute they're jumping down your throat about the facts of life, and the next minute they're taking you to a rock party. Any ideas why that might be?

It sure beats the hell out of me.

That proves my statement about teenagers needing to be called confused. Their parents and lives tend to often leave us that way. When it's all said and done, the parent's are the one's who want to know what's wrong with their kids, without ever thinking it might be them that's wrong.

"Hey, Lewis," called Roy, from the doorway. "Stop day dreaming, and get in here with your beloved guitar."

"On my way," I laughed at his remark, and headed for the door.

"I think your girlfriend is getting a little jealous," he winked. "If you know what I mean?"

"Give it a break," I called. "You're a bass player, not a comedian."

"Right," he said, and walked on into the house.

When Roy started cracking jokes, it meant he was getting nervous. To tell you the truth, I think the three of us were about to blow a gasket.

It was our first live audience. Our very first live concert. That kind of meant life or death for us as a band, if you know what I mean? If we didn't hold up here, we were finished.

Sure. We were okay, when it came to playing to an audience of one. There was nothing to it. Playing to a group of kids we would see in school every day, was a different story. We would have to deal with the failure for the rest of our lives, and that wouldn't be easy.

By now, I had forgotten all about the deal with my Dad. The one about being home by midnight. I was thinking more about how the band was gonna do, and about how the audience would react to us. Dad would have to wait until whenever it came into play.

Right now, I was facing my first real case of stage fright.

We all were.

# CHAPTER THIRTY-NINE

"YOUR DAD SEEMED TO be pretty cool about things," Roy said, when I walked up to our makeshift stage.

"He was acting strange," I said.

"Did he ask about Jenn?"

"Yeah," I said. "I blew around it by saying she was the drummer, and then changed the subject."

"He's gonna find out sooner or later, you know?" Roy stated.

"Jenn wants me to tell him about us tomorrow," I said.

"Write me when you get ungrounded," he smiled.

"Are you still gonna be around in thirty years?" I asked, with a smile of my own.

"Are you kidding?" he laughed. "I'll probably never get out of Parsons."

"I'll just come and see you instead," I said, and slapped him on the back.

"Did you get that problem resolved with the two girls?" he asked, to change the subject.

"Kind of," I replied. "Carol Anne and me, kind of decided what way we needed to go with this. Neither one of us wanted to hurt anyone."

"Then you've still got the problem, right?"

"Not really," I said. "I'm where I want to be, and I think Carol Anne knows that."

"But you're not sure."

"Not really," I said. "The other night when I left Jenn's, I ran into Carol Anne waiting for me in the woods. She made a couple of innocent moves on me, and we ended up kissing."

"Are you crazy?" he asked, with a look of surprise.

"I think so," I said. "To tell you the truth, I kind of liked it."

"I told you that you should date both of them," he smiled, and smacked me on the shoulder.

"I wish it were that easy."

"You're gonna have to resolve this," he said. "Sooner or later, the walls are gonna crash down all around you, and then it's gonna really be over."

"I know," I said, looking over toward where Jenn was talking to a couple of other girls. "The thing is, I think I might be in love with both of them."

"That's it," Roy said, and put up his hands. "I'm staying out of it. I've never been that lucky with two girls at the same time. Therefore, I don't really know what to tell you."

"It's okay," I said. "Sooner or later, I'll figure it out for myself."

"Why don't you just stay with Jenn?" he said.

"You're right," I smiled. "When Carol Anne gets back from Memphis, I'll tell her that I'm going to stay with Jenn."

"And what are you two handsome boys talking about?" Jenn asked, scaring the hell out of me.

"Ryc's Dad," Roy answered. "We were talking about how strange he's been acting."

"It's a phase," Jenn said. "Parents have a million ups and downs, before you get out on your own."

"You've got that right," Roy and I said, at the same time.

It was really good to have someone to talk to. Even if he didn't really know what to say, he did at least help me come to a conclusion of sorts. He also covered our conversation with Jenn, like he was an old pro at cover-ups.

Knowing him, he probably was.

Carol Anne would just have to understand. I loved her. I loved her as a friend, and wanted to remain that way. We had come too close to crossing the line, and taking a chance at destroying the one true thing we really shared together. Nothing was ever fair in love and war, and I wasn't going to take any more chance with our bond.

It was something we had to come to terms with, as we learned to face tomorrow. Carol Anne was bright enough, and strong enough to understand the truth.

I didn't want to lose her because of love.

# CHAPTER FORTY

"YOU GUYS HAD BETTER be good," Donny stated, as we took our places.

"We are," I said, still not quite trusting him.

That was largely due to the fact that my cousin Debbi was nowhere to be seen. I knew that she was still grounded by her father, but knowing Debbi the way I did, I knew she would have found away to be there. That's unless she and the jerk had broken up, for some reason or another.

"What are you guys called, anyway?"

"Two Guys and a Girl," we all chimed at the same time.

"Two Guys and a Girl," he laughed, as he turned around to face the twenty or so other students he had invited. "Fellow Riverside High student body, I give you for your entertainment tonight, 'Two Guys and a Girl.'"

The student body all greeted us with cheers.

"Are you, okay?" I asked Jenn, noticing that she wasn't looking too well.

"Nerves," she smiled.

"This is their very first gig," Donny said. "So don't blame me if they don't measure up."

Everyone clapped their hands, as they took seats wherever they could find a place to sit. I walked up to the mic, and looked around the room at all the faces looking back at me. This was it. Do or die. We were either gonna make it, or fall flat on our faces.

"Hello, everyone," I said into the mic, and closed my eyes.

I lifted my strumming hand into the air, and came down with the opening riff to our first song. Jenn and Roy joined in a moment later, and the show was on the road.

> "Let's heat up the night with fire
> And give into our burning desire
> Let's take our love to the limit
> Cause our heart's are ready to live it
> Let's kiss the moment with love
> And anything else we can think of
> Cause tonight
> Ah, Baby, tonight is our time
> Yes, tonight
> Ah, Baby, tonight you're mine
> I won't take no for answer
> Not even if you were dyin' of cancer
> Love is a one-way street
> When you're dancin' to the beat
> Of two hearts in perfect time
> In love's magical rhyme
> Cause tonight
> Ah, Baby, tonight is our time
> Yes, tonight
> Ah, Baby, tonight you're mine."

The room suddenly exploded with a roar, so loud the music couldn't cover it. Everyone was on there feet clapping their hands and screaming. I don't really know what happened, but my case of stage fright was no longer there. I was riding the first really good time my music had ever given me.

"We did it," Jenn called, from behind me.

I looked over at Roy, who was smiling from ear to ear. I smiled back at him, and went into our next number. There was no stopping us, now that we were on a roll.

The rockin' part of roll that is.

> "What do you think of me?
> When you close your eyes
> What is there for you to see?
> When the light fades and dies
> Don't ask me what I think of you
> You might not like the answer I give
> It doesn't matter if it is true
> As long as you live and let live
> She said she loved me
> But it wasn't true
> Cause she couldn't be
> What she wanted to
> We all look for the right
> Only to find the wrong
> A cross over in the night
> Trying really hard to be strong
> Failing every step of the way
> Like a haunting curse
> With no chance to pray
> For fear of something worse
> She said she loved me
> But it wasn't true
> Cause she couldn't be
> What she wanted to
> No. . . she couldn't be
> What she wanted to."

The place was buzzin' so bad, you would think you were in a bee-hive. I didn't waste anytime to think about what was really going on. I was too strung out on the high to let anything get in the way. How could I? This was the place in life that I wanted to be.

Without stopping, we kicked into the number we had played for Jenn's Dad, and followed it with the tune Carol Anne had been a critic for. With each song, the audience seemed to scream and demand more from us. It was starting to feel like a nonstop roller coaster ride. The kind that kept taking you up and up into the heavens, with the promise of a grand thrill on the way down. I was there riding the ride all the way.

The fifth song we kicked into, was the song my Dad had over heard me playing the other day. Jenn was beating away at her drums, while Roy was getting into the idea of acting like a rock star.

To tell the truth, I believe we were all feeling like rock stars.

We were originally only going to play three songs per-set, but ended up playing six songs instead. Getting caught up in the magic was more powerful than we had ever imagined. In the back of my mind, I was thanking God for letting us know more than six songs.

The last song of that set was a love song I had just written, and the last one we practiced before coming to the show. I'd written it for Jenn, to kind of try to express the way I felt about her.

Her eyes lit up, when I started strumming the cords.

"You are so many things to me
My love, my life, my lady
But most of all
You are my dream
How do I know
This feeling is true
I know by not knowing at all
Maybe it's the way I feel
Maybe it's by the way
You always touch me
And my lonely life
That's how I know
My love, my life, my lady
You are my dream
Just by being you
Oh, I love you
For being you. . ."

At the end of the sixth song, Jenn went into a quick solo, that lead Roy doing a solo on his bass, and finally me on my guitar. I couldn't get over how excited and alive I felt. It was like I had just been born, and the music was my life force.

"Thank you," I said, into the mic, after I finished my solo. "We're going to take a little break, then come back, and play you one more set before we call it quits."

The room screamed again, as we walked out into the audience. There was no stopping the rush we were feeling, as our newfound friends greeted us with their joy.

"You guys were better than I had expected," Donny said, walking up to me, as I made my way around the room.

"Thanks," I said. "I'm glad you liked us."

"The best is yet to come," he smiled, and walked away.

I don't care what you're thinking. I still didn't like the jerk. I just had this gut feeling he was up to something, and that made me uneasy as hell. It was like trying to figure my Dad out, all over again, and it just didn't add up.

I've been around the block enough to know when someone my age was up to something. That look read all over Donny Long. It was a look I didn't trust, or like one bit. It left me with a bad feeling that I was sure I was going to find out tonight.

You know what I mean?

## CHAPTER FORTY-ONE

"Hi," SAID THIS BLONDE headed girl, who came up to me, as I was leaning against the wall.

"Hi," I replied, not all that interested in talking.

I was searching the room for Jenn, and trying to keep my eye on the jerk.

"I think you're really something," she stated. "The way you play your guitar and sing."

"Thanks," I said, taking my eyes off the party, so I could listen to her.

She was my first groupie.

"Whose songs are those, anyway?" she asked. "What band played them originally?"

"They're mine," I said.

"Wow," she smiled. "You'd never know it."

"Is that good?" I asked. "Or is that bad?"

"Good," she replied. "You sound like professionals."

"Thanks again," I said, smiling from ear to ear.

It was one of those ego boost things. If you know what I mean?

"I'm Peggy Sue Gibson," she said, offering me her free hand. The other one was holding a beer.

"I'm Ryc Lewis," I returned the favor, and shook her hand.

"Yeah, I know," she said. "You're Jennifer Tate's boyfriend."

"You know Jenn?" I asked.

"Kinda," she replied. "I know the rest of the gang better. We've all been in one grade or another during the course of going to school."

"I'm still just getting to know people," I confessed. "I really haven't been around most of them that much."

"Why aren't you drinking, like everyone else?" she asked, holding up her can of beer.

"I've got to keep my edge," I replied.

"That's right," she said. "You're gonna be playing again."

"That is if the rest of the band doesn't get drunk first," I smiled; taking note of Roy downing a beer like it was a long drink of water.

"That looks like the way he's headed," she said, noticing Roy herself.

"I'll take a sip of your beer," I said. "If you don't mine?"

"Sure," she said, handing me her beer.

"Ryc?" Jenn called, from across the room. "I have some friends I want you to meet."

"On my way," I called back to her, handing Peggy Sue back her beer, without taking a drink.

"Guess you've got to go?" she asked, taking back her beer.

"Yeah," I said. "Thanks anyway."

"See you around," she said, as I headed toward Jenn.

"Sure," I said, catching the smile in Jenn's eyes.

It was like a lighthouse beam shining through the night, drawing me into safety, from the clutches of a raging storm. It made me understand that although I loved Carol Anne, I knew my heart was with Jenn.

"Who was that?" Jenn asked, after I had reached her.

"Peggy Sue something," I replied. "She was telling me how great the band sounded."

"Yeah," Jenn smiled. "I keep getting the same reaction from everyone that comes up to me. My Dad is gonna have a heart attack when he hears the tape."

"Mine too," I laughed. "Who are these friends you wanted me to meet?"

"Just me," she smiled, and gave me a long kiss. "I just wanted to get you away from that girl."

"Jealous, are we?" I asked, putting her chin into my right hand, and lifting her face up to mine.

"No," she replied, blushing in the cheeks.

"Well, I'm very glad to meet you," I said, kissing her longer than she had kissed me.

"Me too," she said, looking over toward where Roy was still drinking beer. "Do you think we should do our last set? That is, before we don't have a bass player to play with us."

"Might be a good idea," I said, and motioned Roy to the stage.

He quickly downed another beer, as he made his way to the stage.

"By the way," I smiled. "How many of those things have you had?"

"Are you counting?" she asked.

"Not really." I replied.

"Two," she said, and pulled me toward the stage.

Two beers really put her in a good mood. She seemed to be really enjoying herself in a totally different way. Teasingly cute. If you know what I mean? Not so much the pale look she had before we started, but more an alive look.

I liked her that way. It helped to chase away some of the things that were dancing around inside of my head. I guess you could say that it even put me in a better mood about things. Which was probably something I needed at the moment.

It still didn't really hide the fact that she looked a little too pale. I don't really know why, but that part of it still bothered me. There was something to it that I just couldn't shake, or quite put my finger on.

The audience called, so I quickly put it on the back burner, and got ready to sing. Like so many other things in my life at the moment, there wasn't any real time for me to give it any measure of true thought. Right now, I had to put everything into the band, and make sure we stayed on track with the performance.

Sometimes, I think we look to hard to find answers. Answers that usually end up right under our noses. We're just to blind to see that they've always had a life of their own. We just never seem to give them a chance to find us.

That's being part of the human race, right?

Think about that one, and then look under your nose the next time you have a question you can't find an answer to. You just might be surprised at what you find.

I usually am.

# CHAPTER FORTY-TWO

"CAN YOU BELIEVE THESE guys?"
Donny asked, from center stage. "They're really great. Once again,
'Two Guys and a Girl'."

The room exploded into another rage, as we kicked off our first
number of that set. It was still like we had been playing forever, even
with Roy hanging out there in the wind. He never missed a lick. The
audience was like our very own private fan club. One of those things
in life that you would never forget. A best friend, a favorite song, just
whatever hung onto your deepest memories, and would never let go.

> "I had a life long dream
> To go some place I've never seen
> But something always got in the way
> To where I had to stay
> Now I'm walking down memory lane
> Just two steps from going insane
> With a feeling telling me I've got to go
> To the place I thought I would never know

Pick me up, out of my fears
And take me back, to the years
Of my innocent youth
Where I lived by my truth
Pick me up, dry my tears
And wash away all those fears
Somebody told me the other day
That they thought they knew the way
But the moment had escaped them
While caught in a traffic jam
Now they don't see me anymore
Time went and closed that door
And I'm not the same person I used to be
But I'm the one who can no longer see
Pick me up, out of my fears
And take me back, to the years
Of my innocent youth
Where I lived by my own truth
Pick me up, dry my tears
And wash away all those fears. . ."

They were all screaming at us for more. Two girls came up on stage, started kissing me on the face, and damn near scared the hell out of me. Two of the guys in the audience pulled them off, and drug them back out into the audience. Roy was laughing himself half to death, while Jenn looked at me with a smile.

"This is crazy, ain't it?" I asked her.

"It's only rock and roll," she smiled, and started beating her drums into our next song.

"There's a price we pay
For the road we're on
Others' may try to tell you
They know the way
Cause they've already gone
But it isn't true
Cause they, they ain't you
No, No, they ain't you

166

To each his own
And all that kind of stuff
We still choose the way
Walk the path alone
As the moment turns to rust
And yesterday doesn't stay
Cause they, they ain't you
No, no, they ain't you
Oh, they, they ain't you
No, no, they ain't you. . ."

We played three songs that set, because we were running out of material. To be honest with you, we hadn't expected to be as good as they all took us to be. The next time, however, we would be ready.

"We're gonna close with a song that tells the world who we are," I said. "The next master's of the world, when our father's have come and gone, and the next generation steps up to lead the way into tomorrow."

"We are the children of the world
We are the children of the world
And we have the right
The right to fight
So take all your political rules
And stick 'em where they won't shine
Cause we are no longer the fools
Standing in your "got to do this" line
Uncle Sam has lost his pride
While Old Glory looks down in disgrace
With this one hope that will not be denied
Cause one day we will rule the human race
We are the children of the world
We are the children of the world
We're standing up unafraid
To correct the mistakes our father's made
We are the children of the world
We are the children of the world
And we have the right

The right to fight
We are the children of the world
We are the children of the world. . ."


"Thank you," I said, into the mic, and unhooked my guitar. "We loved playing for you, and hope to get to do it aga. . .

"Encore," they all started to yell.

"What do I do?" I asked, Roy and Jenn. "We've played them everything we know."

"Play them one of your songs," Jenn said. "You probably know hundreds of them that we haven't practiced yet."

"Yeah," Roy added. "You know millions of 'em."

"I can't play without you guys," I said, with the house still screaming for more.

"We don't have to play with you," Jenn said. "You're the band. We're just a part of it."

"Yeah, Ryc," Roy said. "You are the band. You saw how they were reacting to you."

"I'm not gonna play without you guys," I stated.

"You're what they wanna hear, Ryc," Jenn said, and stood up from her drums.

"I'm not playing without you guys," I said again.

"It's not gonna happen," Jenn said. "This time you're on your own."

"Sorry," Roy smiled, and stepped up to the mic. "Ryc here, is gonna play you a song by himself."

The place exploded again, and my stage fright feeling was back. Playing with the band was one thing. Playing alone was a totally different one.

"Good luck," Jenn said, kissed me, and walked off stage with Roy.

"Well," I smiled, at everyone who had their eyes staring at me up there on that great big lonely stage. "I guess this is it."

I closed my eyes, and started singing.


"Now that we are
There's gonna be no more
Wishing on a star
This is what love is for
I lost you once, I won't again

Not after where we've been
We were meant to be
And together we will see
That love is so right
Like the birth of a new days light
I'll be the one
To make your love live on
You were too blind to see
That love was always me
I lost you once, I won't again
Not after where we've been
Cause what we share now
Was always meant somehow
I lost you once, I won't again
Not after where we've been
I lost you once, I won't again
Not after where we've been. . ."

The place was completely silent, as I strummed my guitar to a slow
fade. It was the first time I had ever felt so in control of anything. Me,
Richart Drake Lewis, the nobody super king of the born losers.

"Thank you," I said, and walked off stage to the woman of my
dreams. Miss Jennifer La' Nette Tate. The girl standing near the kitchen
door, smiling back at me.

The room exploded.

It's funny how you can figure somethings out. How you can know
who that one special person in the world is. How it can wrap you up
inside of yourself, and finally make you believe in the impossible
dream.

Too bad all things weren't that easy.

# CHAPTER FORTY-THREE

THE PARTY WAS COMING to an end, as the guests started to leave. I hadn't seen Jenn in over half an hour, and the last time I did see her, she was about three sheets into the wind. I, myself, knew better. My Dad would be sure to check me out, when I got home. So I stuck to straight soda, during the rest of the party.

I went into the kitchen for another soda, when I saw Jenn standing outside on the back deck. She was alone, with the jerk. He was trying very unsuccessfully to put the moves on her. At first, I thought it was kind of funny, even though I still didn't like the idea.

"What do you see in that Indian freak, anyway?" he asked her, putting his arm around her shoulder.

"To start with," Jenn said, pushing his arm off her shoulder. "He's not a jerk like you are."

"I'm a jerk?" he asked.

"Yeah," Jenn said, stepping away from him.

"Why am I a jerk?" he asked, grabbing her by the arm, and pulling her back to the rail.

"One, because you have a girlfriend," she said. "Two, because Ryc is just inside the house, and you could care less about his feelings."

"First of all," he smiled. "My girlfriend dumped me. As for your boyfriend in the house, he wouldn't know what to do with a girl like you."

"Really," she smiled. "I think Ryc and I have a great relationship. Someone like you could probably learn a few things from a man like him."

"Give me a break," he snapped.

"Give me a break," Jenn said. "I don't like you, and I don't think you need to be making passes at me."

"What are you gonna do?" he asked, with a devilish grin. "Tell your Mr. Kung Fu that I've been trying to get into your pants?"

"As a matter of fact," Jenn said, stepping away from him once more. "I think maybe that's exactly what I am gonna do."

"Bring him on," Donny said. "I'm ready to take the little freak out."

"I think maybe we should be going," I suggested, stepping out to join them.

"I agree," said Jenn, coming toward me.

"Not quite so fast," said Donny, grabbing her by the arm again, and jerking her back to him.

By now, several of the remaining guests were watching what was going on. Most of which were the jerk's truest friends.

"Leave me alone," Jenn screamed.

"Don't push your luck, Long," I said, going naturally into a fighting stand.

"Ryc?" Roy said, stepping up beside me. "Maybe you should re-think this."

"It's too late for that," I smiled, and gave Roy a wink.

"Give it up, Lewis," Donny said. "I talked to your stupid cousin, and she told me that your Kung Fu shit was just a story you guys came up with to keep me from kicking your ass."

"You may be surprised," I said, silently thanking Debbi for pulling it off. It served the jerk right, not to know what he was in for.

"Let's see what you're gonna do," He said, and slid his hand into Jenn's blouse, and started playing with her right breast. "Does this make you mad enough to fight for her?"

My eyes turned red, I'm sure, as my anger boiled to a rage within my blood filled veins. I'm sorry, but the son of a bitch passed the limit of my tolerance.

"Now," I said, motioning him to me, in much the same manner as Bruce Lee would have done.

"Right on," he said, pushing Jenn away from him so hard, it ripped her blouse half off of her, as she hit the deck at full force.

"Don't kill him," Roy said from behind me.

I let Donny take the first punch. He missed, as I sidestepped it.

"You just got lucky," he snapped, and caught his balance.

"Maybe I did," I smiled, and went back into my stand.

"Let's just leave," Jenn said.

"I wish it were that easy," I said.

"You're not going anywhere," Donny spit. "Not until we settle this, right here and now."

"Don't say we didn't warn you," Jenn said, and stepped behind Roy.

"C'mon," I smiled. "Kick my ass, Donny."

I let him take the second punch. He missed that one too, as I stepped back, and let him stumble on by me. When he caught his balance, I jumped up into the air in a spinning kick, and made contact with the side of his face.

"Had enough?" I asked, as he got back on his feet, holding the side of his face.

"You still just got lucky," he slurred, spitting blood, as he made another charge for me.

This time, I grabbed him by the arm, spun him around, kicked him three times in the nose, and watched him fall face first into the deck. He made a few silent mumbles, and was out cold. Remember that I did tell him he might be surprised.

"You didn't have to do that to him," Jenn snapped.

"What else was I gonna do?" I asked. "You know he wasn't going to let us go, without a fight."

"You could have killed him," she said.

"Yeah, I could have," I said. "But I didn't."

"Men," she snapped, and took off through the woods toward her house.

"Jenn?" I called, but she kept going.

"Go after her," Roy said. "I'll make sure everything gets loaded onto your Dad's truck."

"Thanks," I said, patting him on the back, before I took off.

I found myself at a loss for words. I hoped she really didn't think I was going to let him get away with what he did. No. No way was it happening. Donny had it coming. I felt it all night. To tell you the truth, the jerk probably had it coming for years.

I told you so in the beginning. There was something that just wasn't right about the way Donny was acting, and this getting us there at his house. We would have probably never gone, if it weren't for the concert. I knew he was up to something.

Okay, okay, I was mad. I was mad at Donny for what he had done, what he had changed the best night of my life into, and for what he had provoked. I was also kind of mad at Jenn for the way she acted when the fight was over, and for taking off the way she did.

I was defending her honor. Isn't that what the boyfriend is supposed to do? I'm sure as hell not gonna let him take advantage of her, and that's exactly what he was doing when he stuck his hand into her blouse.

I had every right to be mad. Every right in the world. If I had to do it all over again, I would do exactly the same thing. I'd done it even if she weren't my girlfriend.

Why did she act that way?

## CHAPTER FORTY-FOUR

I FOUND HER SITTING in the woods at the Thinking Rock. It was kind of ironic that she'd end up there of all places.

"Hey," I said, walking up behind her.

"Leave me alone, Ryc," she said.

"I can't," I said, putting my arm around her, as I sat down beside her.

"You didn't need to do that to him," she said, moving away from me.

"He didn't need to do what he did either," I stated.

"He was drunk," she said, with tears in her eyes.

"He also had this whole thing planned," I said. "That's why he broke up with Debbi."

"I'm sorry," she cried. "I just don't like it when people fight."

"Neither do I," I said, as she got up, and stepped away from me. "I'm trained to know that I'm not learning how to fight, but how not to fight."

"So why did you do it?" she asked.

"Because I love you," I said, walking over to the edge of the cliff.

Neither one of us said a word for several minutes, as I stood with my back to her, watching one of the barges float down the river. If it weren't for the soft sound of her breathing, you would almost think I was standing there alone.

"I love you too," she whispered.

"I'm sorry about the night," I replied, turning around to face her.

She was standing there topless, with her jeans unsnapped.

"Make love to me, Ryc," she said, with tears streaming down her cheeks.

"Jenn," I said, taking her into my arms. "I would love to make love to you, but I can't. Not tonight."

"Why?" she asked, looking into my eyes.

"You've been drinking," I said, with tears of my own, forming in the corners of my eyes. "I'd feel like I was taking advantage of you."

"It's not fair," she cried, in a whisper.

"I'm sorry, Jenn," I said, as she pushed away from me.

"It's just not fair," she said again, grabbed her blouse off the ground, and took off running toward her house.

"Jenn," I whispered, as she vanished from my sight.

I didn't know what to do. I just stood there looking into the darkness. My tears came, but I didn't cry. I just hurt inside, like I've never hurt before. It felt like I was carrying the weight of the world upon my shoulders, with no way to shake it off.

"JENNIFER!" I screamed, and sat down on the Thinking Rock.

What was I gonna do? I asked myself. What was I gonna do to change all this?

That's when I felt it under my hand. Jenn's bra. She had forgotten to take it with her. It was the last thing I needed to find.

Oh, God, I thought. I'll never be able to explain this to her father, if I took it to her. He'd know that she had been drinking, probably think that I had tried to force myself on her, by the way she had come in, and have me arrested for an attempt of rape.

Taking it to her was the wrong answer. I'd just have to wait until it all blew over, or she called me. I'd give it to her then.

What if she didn't call? What if she never wanted to see me again? What was I gonna do? How could I ever face another day without her?

Someone, please, shoot me, and get it over with.

I stuck the bra into my jacket pocket, and took off walking in the other direction. I didn't know where I was going, and at that moment I didn't really care. I was frozen inside myself, and couldn't feel or think about anything.

I also forgot what time it was.

# CHAPTER FORTY-FIVE

DAD WAS WAITING UP for me, when I got home. It was three-thirty in the morning, and he was not at all happy about it.

"Where the hell have you been?" he snapped, as I opened the door.

"Walking," I said, because it was the truth.

"Walking?" he repeated, in the form of a question. "Do you really expect me to believe that you've been out walking?"

"Yes," I said, and he grabbed me by the neck.

"Why would you be out walking until three-thirty in the damn morning?" he asked, spitting in my face, as he ran his mouth a full speed.

"I had a lot of thinking to do," I said. "The God's honest truth is, I just kind of spaced the time."

"No one just spaces three and a half hours," he snapped, and threw me up against the wall." "Not without a really good reason, and I doubt very seriously that you have one."

"I have one," I said, picking myself up off the floor.

"Who is she?" he asked, grabbing me again.

"Dad?" I pleaded, as he slammed me against the wall again.

That's when the bra fell out of my jacket pocket. It was also the moment his eyes just about jumped completely out of his head. He smacked me up beside the head so hard I saw stars, then threw me up against the wall again, and picked up the bra.

"What the hell is this?" he asked, daring me to lie to him about it.

"It's a bra," I replied.

Smack! He hit me up beside the face again, knocking me to the ground, and started kicking me in the side. It hurt so bad, it brought tears to my eyes.

"Let me explain," I cried.

"Let's hear it," he snapped, as he grabbed me by the hair, and threw me onto the couch. "I really want to hear what kind of lie you have to get out of this."

Mom was standing in the hallway, near the living room entrance, biting her lip. She knew not to say a word to him, when he was that mad.

"It belongs to Jenn," I said. "You know, the drummer in my band."

"I figured there was more to you two then what you were saying," he said, pacing the floor like a wild animal. "I could see it in the way she looked at you."

"Donny," I said, looking him in the eye.

"Donny who?" he asked.

"The guy who gave the party we played for," I said.

"He made a couple of really lewd passes toward her, and I kicked his ass."

"Over a girl?" he asked, getting down into my face.

"Yes," I said. "She's my girlfriend, not his."

"Your girlfriend?" he asked, and pushed me into the couch.

"Yes," I confessed. "I didn't let you know, because I knew you would act this way."

Smack! He hit me in the mouth with his fist, and I tasted blood. I hated it, when I tasted blood, because it scared me. I was afraid that I was going to lose control, and start hitting him back. Fearing that once I got started, I wouldn't know when to stop.

"How the hell did you end up with her bra?" he asked, standing over me again.

"Jenn got mad at me for beating Donny up," I said. "She took off through the woods, and I followed her. When I caught up with her, we talked about what happened, and then kind of made up."

"So then you made love to her," he stated, as if he knew. Glaring at me with eyes that could cut through stone. "What'd you do, keep the bra as a trophy?"

"No," I replied, with my anger starting to show." "She was drunk, and I didn't want to waste what I shared with her, on a moment like that. I have more respect for myself and her to take advantage of the opportunity."

Everything froze to a total silent, as I watched the expression on his face.

"Then how did you end up with her bra?" he asked, in an even tone.

"She took it off," I said, still watching him. "She asked me to make love to her. When I told her that I couldn't, for the same reasons I just told you, she got upset, and took off running toward her house. I found the bra, stuck it in my pocket, and decided to give it to her when things cooled off."

"You're telling me the truth, aren't you?" he asked, in a tone that took me by surprise.

"I always tell you the truth," I said. "I was late, because I honestly spaced the time. I had a lot of thinking to do, and just took off walking."

"I need to let this all set in," he said. "Until then, you're not to go around her."

"Her father probably won't let me see her anyway," I said. "After what happened, she probably feels the same way, and doesn't want to see me either."

"Go to bed," he said. "We'll continue this later."

"What about Jenn's drums?" I asked, walking toward the hallway.

"I'll take them to her, when I pickup the truck," he stated." "I want to talk to her parents about all of this."

"Her father," I corrected him. "Her mother died of cancer three years ago."

"Just the same," he said. "I think he and I need to talk about this, and see where we are going to go with it."

"Great," I said. "Now I know he'll never let me see her again."

"As of right now," Dad smiled. "You don't have a girlfriend."

"Don't you think that should be something Jenn and I decide for ourselves?" I asked, hoping I wasn't crossing the line.

"No, I don't," he replied.

I went to bed, but didn't go to sleep. I was too worked up to allow myself the luxury of being able to go to sleep. The thing with Jenn, the fight with Dad, and what lie ahead, were just too much for me to cope with.

I tried to think, but soon found that I couldn't. There were just too many what ifs dancing around every answer I came up with.

Instead of thinking, I lay in the still darkness, staring out my window, and cried like a baby.

It wasn't fair.

None of it was fair. Why me? I wondered. I did all the right things an honorable man would have done, and still I'm the one who got in trouble. What did I do, to bring all this crashing down upon my head?

I asked, but the answers never came.

# CHAPTER FORTY-SIX

I WAS IN MY room, working on a new song, with one of my other guitars, when Dad came home from Jenn's. I hadn't left it all day, and half-expected him to come in bragging about what he and Mr. Tate had talked about.

Only, he didn't. He didn't come to my door, until an hour or so later.

"Ryc?" he asked, from the other side of the door. "Can I come in?"

"Yeah," I called, and stopped playing.

"What was that song you were playing?" he asked, shutting the door behind him.

"Just one of my songs," I said.

"Would you play it for me?" he asked.

"Why?" I asked, surprised that he asked to hear it. Only once before had he ever asked to hear one of my songs, and that was just a few days before.

"Because I would like to hear what you really sound like," he replied. "Your Mr. Tate seems to think you have a very talented gift."

"You might not like what it says," I said. "The songs I write are either about being in love, or escaping into another world."

"I grew up in the '50's," he said. "I kind of know what being a teen-ager, and what rock and roll are all about."

"Okay," I said, and started playing.

> "I know the story all too well
> It's been through heaven and hell
> Once it was all there is
> And now it's the first thing you miss
> Ride train ride
> To a place beyond the sun
> Ride train ride
> To a place where victories are won
> Ride train ride
> All my bags are packed to go
> To where I don't know
> I just know I'm on my way
> Because I can't stay,
> Ride train ride
> To a place beyond the sun
> Ride train ride
> To a place where victories are won
> Ride train ride
> Tired of all the voices
> Reminding me of the wrong choices
> And dreams that come to an end
> Every single place I've been
> Ride train ride
> Oh, ride train ride."

"I really didn't know you were so good," he said, after I put a finish on the song.

"You never listened," I said.

"I've heard you," he said. "I just never knew how serious you were about it."

"Well," I smiled. "It's my dream."

"Are you trying to say something with this song?" he asked, and I knew before he did, that he would.

"No," I said. "It's just a song that expresses how teens feel today."

"I talked to Jenn's father," he said, looking the other way.

"What did he say?"

"We both agreed that maybe the two of you should not see each other for a while," he replied, looking back at me. "Besides, he said that she was really sick, and that he didn't think she needed any visitors right now."

"It's probably a hang over," I smiled.

"That's what I thought," he said. "Only that's not the way he put it."

"What do you mean?" I asked.

"I'm not sure," he said. "If I were guessing, I say she had one of those new flu bugs that's going around these days."

"When can I see her again?" I asked.

"Maybe in a week or two," he replied.

"Is that how long I'm grounded for?"

"No," he said, and opened the door. "You're not grounded this time. Aside from not seeing your girlfriend."

I couldn't figure it out. I really expected him to be really pissed off, and keep me grounded for the rest of my natural life. Instead, he kind of blew it off, as if nothing had ever happened. He even called her my girlfriend.

What's up with that?

Maybe my telling him the truth worked. Maybe he really was trying to understand me. Maybe he was listening to what I said, instead of just hearing it?

Like I said, I just couldn't figure it out. He was acting really odd about the whole thing, and that in a way made you want to wonder about it.

So why kick a gifted horse in the mouth? Things were working better for me, now that I decided not to try and worm out of what had happened. I really didn't know why I didn't try to come up with another angle to get myself out of it. Hell, maybe I was changing to.

It bothered me that I couldn't see Jenn. But then, I also understood why. Maybe it was the best thing for both of us?

Like all things these days, I didn't really know.

183

# CHAPTER FORTY-SEVEN

"YOU ACTUALLY TURNED MAKING love to her down?" Roy asked, after I told him the story.

"I didn't want to feel guilty about having sex with her when she'd been drinking," I said. "My feelings for her are more than just sexual."

"I can't believe you turned it down," he replied, shaking his head. "What if you never get another shot at it?"

"Then I guess it's my loss," I said.

"Drinking or not, I don't think I would have turned it down." Roy said. "Not with a chic that looks as good as Jenn."

"That's the difference between us," I said. "I don't mean anything bad about it, but I can."

"So when do you get to see her again?"

"Two weeks," I replied. "Her Dad says that she's sick, right now."

"It's probably just a hangover," Roy smiled. "She was knock'em out pretty good there toward the end."

"What about you?" I smiled. "If I remember right, you were drinking enough to sink a battleship."

"I never have a hangover," he smiled.

"Did you listen to the tape yet?" I asked, because it was his reel to reel we recorded the show on, and I knew that he would have taken it home with him.

"It was great," he said, smiling from ear to ear. "We sounded like professionals."

"When do I get to hear it?"

"I'll bring it by this weekend," he said. "I just came to get my bass, before my Dad has a fit. He says that there's too much money wrapped up in it, to just leave it anywhere."

"I've heard that one before," I laughed. "It's like we're not allowed to make our own judgment as to whom we can trust, and who we can't."

"You've got that right," Roy laughed with me. "My Dad wouldn't trust a fart, even if he were the one who let it."

"That's Bad," I replied, laughing even harder.

"Does this mean the band is history?" he asked, picking up his base, and amp. "Seeing how things are going right now?"

"At least for the next two weeks," I replied. "After that, who knows? You and I can still work on things, if you want?"

"Sure," he replied. "Only it's not going to be the same."

"What do you mean?"

"The three of us had a special kind of magic going," he replied. "I think we'd end up missing something."

"Yeah," I said. "The drummer."

"You've got that right," Roy laughed.

"It may stop the band for a while," I said. "But it's not gonna stop me from writing. If I couldn't write my songs, I'd go insane."

"I hope not," Roy said. "You write some really good shit."

"Thanks," I said. "You even play a pretty mean bass. Even when you're a couple of sheets into the wind."

"It's my job," he smiled, and started toward the door.

We talked until Roy's Dad was ready to go. My Dad had agreed to build a utility room onto the side of their house. Dad was one of those part-time carpenters that did side jobs like that on weekends. Which was perfectly all right with me, because it would mean Roy and I could hangout together on the days we were there.

I'm not sure if it was because summer was slowly coming to an end, or if it was because school was getting ready to start again, but something was changing in the air that I couldn't quite put my finger on. It was like everything would slow down to almost a crawl, then speed back up to one of those "what did I miss?" moments, and then back again. It was something that just attacked my thoughts, when I gave it the consideration it begged for.

My life was starting to change, right before my eyes, and without me.

I didn't really see much of anyone over the next two weeks that I waited to see Jenn again, except for Roy, who was out riding his bike a lot. Carol Anne was in Memphis again, Debbi was in Arkansas with her Dad, and Jenn was, as you know, off limits.

I did get wind that Donny was going around telling everyone that the only reason I whipped him, was because he had been drinking. I naturally put the word out that if he wanted to try sober, he knew where I lived, and that I would be waiting for him.

He never came around.

# CHAPTER FORTY-EIGHT

ON THE LAST DAY of my not being able to see Jenn, I called to see if I could talk to her. Mr. Tate answered the phone, and told me that she wasn't receiving any phone calls or visitors. It didn't stop me from trying, or trying to find out why.

"Is it because of what happened at the party?" I asked, praying that it wasn't.

"No," he replied. "Kids your age make mistakes all the time. Jenn's just been really sick lately, and not really up to it."

"Will you tell her that I called?"

"Yes," he replied. "She'll be glad that you did."

Okay, I thought, as I rode my dirt bike down to the Floating Store. If everything was okay about what happened, why was I still not allowed to see her? She's been sick, but is that really an excuse?

Maybe she didn't want to see me anymore, and Mr. Tate didn't have the heart to tell me? Maybe this, and maybe that? It was just about enough to drive a person insane. I just didn't know what to make of it.

I guess sometimes we all get a little weird.

"Hey, Lewis?" called the voice of Roy Miller.

"Roy," I called back.

"What are you up to?" he asked, after I had pulled up beside him, and cut the engine to my bike.

"Gettin' a cold drink," I replied. "Want one?"

"Why not?" he said, following me down to the Floating Store. "Have you been able to see Jenn yet?"

"No," I replied to his question. "Her Dad says that she's still sick, and that she's not seeing anyone at the moment."

"Ain't that a bit strange?" he asked, as I paid for our drinks. "What kind of sickness lasts for over two weeks?"

"I don't know," I replied, as we walked back to our bikes.

"You should have made love to her," he razzed.

"I'm beginning to think that maybe you're right," I said, and punched him in the arm.

"Hey," called the voice of the blonde I talked to at the concert.

"Peggy Sue, right?" I said, still not remembering her last name.

"Yeah," she smiled. "How's it going?"

"Okay," I said. "How's it going with you?"

"Just fine," she replied. "When are you guys gonna play again?"

"We're not sure," Roy smiled.

"That's only because no one has bothered asking us yet," I added.

"That's too bad," she said. "You guys are really good."

"Thanks," Roy and I said at the same time.

"You really took care of Donny," she said. "Jerks like him need to be knocked down a few notches."

"He just pushed my last button," I smiled.

"He sure must have pushed it good," she said. "No one has really seen him since that night, and those that have keep saying that he thinks you're the one in hiding."

"Do you see me hiding?" I asked, noticing that Roy had walked away from us.

"No," she replied.

"If he really wants to find me," I said. "He knows where to look."

"Well," she smiled. "It was nice to see you again."

"The same," I replied.

"See ya around," she said, and headed down to the Floating Store.

"Sure," I said, and headed over to where Roy was waiting for me at the bikes.

"You're not messin' around with Peggy Sue Gibson, are you?" he asked, with a worried look.

"No," I said, kind of puzzled. "I met her at the concert, and she stopped to talk."

"Make sure that's all you do," Roy said.

"Why?" I asked, wondering what this was all about.

"First of all," he said. "You're already having enough trouble with the two girls you've got hanging on you as it is. Another one would only screw you up more, and she's not the kind of girl you want to get caught up with."

"Enough said," I smiled.

"Good," he said. "I was beginning to think that I was going to have to be your baby-sitter."

"Let's not go that far, okay?" I laughed. "My Dad takes care of that problem all too well. If you know what I mean?"

"Are you kidding me?" he laughed.

He never did say exactly what it was, but by his reaction, I was sure I could eventually figure it out for myself. There was something about Miss Peggy Sue that he knew, and that he wasn't too fond of. I didn't really press it, because I didn't really want to know, and the only girl I had on my mind at the moment was Jenn.

Roy and I took off on our bikes, and rode them up until the time he had to head for home. When he was gone, I went into my room to work on a love song for Jenn, and think about what was going on around me. The song was actually an "I love you" and "I'm sorry" song that I hoped would reach out, and break down any walls that might have been put up.

That is if I ever got to play it for her.

With that in mind, I decided to give trying to get in touch with her a rest for a couple of days. By then, hopefully, she would be over whatever it was that was making her sick. If not, I was going to demand to see her, or at least get some kind of answer.

I mean, why not? She was my girlfriend, and I had a right to know what was really going on. Didn't I? I also had the right to know if she'd broken up with me. There are some honorable things about being in love that still meant something to some of us.

In my heart, I believed that was true about me and Jenn.

## CHAPTER FORTY-NINE

"WHY ARE YOU AVOIDING me?" I asked Carol Anne, one afternoon when I caught her heading toward the Floating Store.

"I'm not avoiding you," she snapped. "I've just got things to do."

"What's happened to us, Carol Anne?" I asked, grabbing her by the arm. "One day we're secretly in love with each other, and the next day it's like we don't even remember fighting to keep it under control."

"That's why it's under control," she said, and jerked away from me. "Now if you'll excuse me I'm running a little behind."

"What about me?" I asked, and knew it was a stupid thing to do.

"It's not about you," she said, and left me where I was standing.

"I know it's not about me," I called after her, but she kept going. "I'm sorry, Carol Anne. I just don't know what to do."

She stopped for a moment, looked over her shoulder, and just stared at me. It felt like she wanted to say something, but the words never came.

Like myself, it looked like she might have been crying.

Why was she crying? What was she crying about?

It must have been as hard on her as it was me realizing the truths that haunted us. I wondered if it were the same way with Jenn? Was Jenn feeling the same way I was, or was all this now some kind of mean joke?

God, I didn't know what to think. I didn't know where to turn, or even who to ask for that matter.

I felt so lost.

# CHAPTER FIFTY

IT WAS RAINING REALLY hard, when I chanced to call Jenn again. It had been close to three weeks since I had seen or talked to her, and I was starting to get really worried about things. I was really hating all the weird ideas that were jumping into my head, and knew that I had to get somewhere with this.

"Hello, Mr. Tate," I said, after he had answered the phone. "May I speak to Jenn?"

"I'm afraid. . ." he said, and then didn't finish.

"Is that Ryc?" I heard a very fragile voice ask in the background. Jenn's voice.

"Yes," he replied.

"I'll speak to him," she said, while I listened.

"Are you sure you're up to it?" he asked. "You really shouldn't be up now."

"Please, Daddy?" Jenn asked.

"Okay," Mr. Tate said, as I waited to hear her speak to me. "But not for very long."

"Ryc?" she asked.

"I'm here," I said, in almost a whisper.

"I can't talk very long," she stated, with a voice that sounded very weak.

"How have you been?" I asked.

"Not so good," she said. "How have you been?"

"Okay," I replied, with tears running down my cheeks. "I've just been missing you more than anything these days."

"Yes," she said, and I could tell she was crying as well. "I've missed you too."

"Will I get to see you again?" I asked.

"You'll know when," she said.

"Honey," Mr. Tate said in the background. "You probably should be getting back to bed now. You've been up way too long as it is."

"Okay, Daddy," she said, and there was a short pause. "I have to go now."

"Okay," I said.

"I love you, Ryc," she whispered.

"I love you too, Jenn," I said, with my heart pounding over time inside my chest.

"I know," she said, and the line went dead.

This wasn't right. How could she be so sick, and for so long? Maybe it was some kind of mono, or pneumonia? I've heard that they lasted forever sometimes.

I don't know about pneumonia, but I've heard that mono can be spread from person to person, and if that's the case. It would explain why I've not been allowed to see her.

Why won't someone tell me what the hell it is? I'm tired of beating my head against the wall, and not getting anywhere.

At least she did get to talk to me. She also told me that she loved me, and that she knew I loved her. That's got to count for something.

Unless it was all for show.

I don't really believe that. Not Jenn. She would never take me on that kind of ride. It just hurts really bad. Especially, when you get no answers to help you deal with things. In fact, it hurts so bad, it alters the way you are, and the way you think.

It makes you really angry.

# CHAPTER FIFTY-ONE

CAROL ANNE WENT TO Memphis and came back from Memphis a few days later, but she never came around to see me. It was like I had become a total stranger to her. It made me feel that what we were to each other was no longer true, that we had somehow drifted too far apart, and I no longer was the love interest of her life. Not even her friend.

It scared me. I hated feeling that way. It's like the entire world was turning against me, and taking the most important people in my life with it. I really, really hated feeling that way. Like I had been robbed of something I didn't know how to get it back.

That's what scared me the most.

I did, however, see Carol Anne on several occasions. She was headed toward Jenn's, and staying there for hours at a time, while Mr. Tate left on errands. I know this to be true, because I followed her there.

I decided to call the next time I saw Carol Anne headed toward Jenn's. If Carol Anne still felt anything for me, she would let me come down to see Jenn, after Mr. Tate had gone for the day. It was the only way I believed I would get to see her.

"Carol Anne," I said, into the phone after she had answered.

"Ryc?" she asked, a little surprised. "What do you want?"

"I would like to talk to Jenn," I replied.

"I can't let you do that," she said. "Besides, she's a sleep."

"A sleep?" I asked. "Is she still sick?"

"You might say that," Carol Anne said.

"You're on the level, right?" I asked.

"I've got no reason to lie to you," she replied.

"Can I come down to see for myself?" I asked. "It's been like forever since I saw her last, and it would mean a lot to me."

"I really would like to let you," Carol Anne said. "But I promised Jenn and her father that I wouldn't for any reason."

"Why?"

"Jenn doesn't want you to see her sick like this," Carol Anne replied. "She doesn't look to healthy right now, and she's not in the best of spirits."

"It's not gonna change how I feel about her," I said.

"I know it won't," Carol Anne said. "Look. It's just a girl thing."

"Well," I said, a little colder than I wanted to. "This girl's thing is about to drive me nuts."

"I know it is, Ryc," she said. "I feel for you."

"That's not good enough, Carol Anne," I said, as tears rolled down my face,

"I'm sorry, Ryc," Carol Anne said. "It's just that I promised them I wouldn't let you come down, and I have to keep my word."

"What's wrong with her?"

"It's like mono," she replied, after a long pause.

"Why are you avoiding me?" I asked, changing the subject.

"Because of what's going on right now," she said. "I could never trust myself face to face with you. You make me give in."

"Please, Carol Anne," I begged.

"I can't," she said, and hung up the phone.

I could tell that she was crying to.

I hung up the phone, and laid back on my bed. I had to chase away my tears, and think about this a little more. It was like mono, she had said. Okay, mono is a really bad case of the flu. At least that's the way I've understood it to be. What's worse than mono? Pneumonia. That's was worse than anything. So why wasn't she in the hospital? Didn't people go to the hospital when they had pneumonia? What was Mr. Tate thinking?

Okay, maybe it wasn't as bad as that yet.

This wasn't right. Nothing about it was right. So what was the real deal here? Why wasn't I allowed to at least see her? Why was I being denied, and Carol Anne could come and go as she pleased? One way or another, I was going to find out, and nothing was going to stop me.

Nothing.

Sooner or later, they were going to have to break, and when they did I was going to be there. They had to let me see her. If not that, then they were going to have to tell me what was really going on. There would be no other way around it.

It wasn't fair. I had done nothing wrong. In fact, I had acted like a gentleman, and not taken advantage of her. So why was I being punished, and not allowed to see or talk to her? None of this really added up.

Not one single bit of it.

If I had done something wrong, I could understand the reason. The only thing was, I had not done anything wrong. Surely that has to count for something.

Maybe Roy was right. Maybe I should have made love to her. At least I wouldn't be out here in the limbo part of the Twilight Zone, trying to figure it all out by myself, and going nuts at the same time.

It was starting to make me get really mad, and mad wasn't something anyone wanted to see. It was the worse possible thing for them to do.

Seriously.

## CHAPTER FIFTY-TWO

"How ya doin'?" Dad asked, late one night while I was playing my guitar on the front porch.

"Makin' it, I guess," I replied, and stopped playing.

He wasn't being himself, and that kind of bugged me. Mostly because I didn't know what to make of him either.

"It'll get easier with time," he said. "It always does."

"What gets easier?" I asked, because he wasn't making himself very clear.

"Dealing with life," he replied. "The older you get the easier somethings become."

"Yeah," I said. "Getting there's the problem."

"Was that song you were playing something you wrote?" he asked, changing the subject.

"Yeah," I said. "Why the sudden interest in the things I'm doing?"

"Nothing really," he replied, and set down next to me. "I guess maybe I'm trying not to miss anymore of who you really are."

What was this? This wasn't him at all.

"All you've got to do is look," I said.

"How about starting by letting me hear that song all the way through," he said, and tapped my guitar.

"Sure," I said, "but you're confusing the hell out of me."

"Sometimes we open our eyes a little too late, Ryc," he said. "I'm trying really hard to open mine before I get to that point."

"Okay," I said, because I didn't know what else to say.

"I didn't see it before," he said. "But I think your music is who you really are, or it best illustrates who you are."

"Mom would disagree with you," I said. "She thinks my art is who I am."

"Maybe to her it is," he smiled. "So how about that song?"

"Sure," I said, and started strumming. "Unlike the other song you listened to the other day, it's about the way I see things right now."

"See what I mean?" he said, with a smile. "Your music is who you are."

"Maybe it is," I agreed, and kicked the song into gear.

> "Never saw it coming
> I was too blind to see
> Kind of been out running
> From my own destiny
> Didn't know my own heart
> From all the temptations around
> But I should have known from the start
> Your love was taking me without a sound
> Your love's taking me
> Down a road I've never been
> And as far as I can see
> That's the way it's gonna be from here on end
> Just the way it should be
> Down a road I've never been
> When the truth hit me in the face
> It was too late to make a stand
> Fate had taken you from the human race
> And left me where I am
> Cause my heart won't let you go
> It keeps you forever inside
> Though I've moved on I want you to know

What I feel for you will never be denied
Your love's taking me
Down a road I've never been
And as far as I can see
That's the way it's gonna be from here on end
Just the way it should be
Down a road I've never been
Your love's taking me
Down a road I've never been
And as far as I can see
That's the way it's gonna be from here on end
Just the way it should be
Down a road I've never been."

"Just what are you trying to say with the song, Ryc," he asked, after I had finished playing it.

"All the things that I've experienced lately have a lot to do with the way I feel about Jenn," I replied. "All those feelings have taken me down many roads I've never been, and right now I feel a little bit lost."

"Things will work themselves out," he said, and patted me on the back.

"Yeah," I said, looking up at him. "But are they gonna be the same?"

"What do you mean?"

"Right now it's like the world has taken her away from me," I said. "I don't know what things are gonna be like after all this, because being apart this long is bound to change things. What I do know is how I feel about her now, and even if it's not the same those feelings will always be inside of me."

"It's really hard to love someone that way," he said. "Because no matter what you do, they'll never be able to see it the way your heart does."

"So is that wrong?"

"No," he replied. "Loving someone that much is never wrong. It's just a lonely place to be."

"You've got that right," I said, with a little laugh.

"That sounds like a song title," he said, and stood up to leave. "Whatever you do, don't let it change who you are."

"That's the problem, Dad," I said. "I think it already has."

199

"Maybe on the outside," he said. "But not on the inside where it counts the most. That part of you will always show through. Even when people take you down roads you've never been."

"Yeah," I said, really feeling like I was going to cry, and trying really hard to keep from doing so.

"Follow your heart, Ryc," he said. "It'll show you the way you need to go every time."

"Yeah," I said. "Because my head keeps making a mess of things."

"That's the way it works," he said, and left me alone.

You talk about strange. Now that was really strange. Every time he acts like that, it's strange. Before I never took him serious, but this time was different. There was something hanging in the air that I wasn't quite catching, and as far as I knew probably never would.

Sooner or later I usually did, but not this time.

This time was different. Things were different. We were different.

# CHAPTER FIFTY-THREE

"WHAT'S WRONG WITH YOU, Ryc?"
Mom asked, coming into my room a few days later. "You don't play
your guitar, you don't eat, and I know you don't sleep."

She was right. Ever since that talk with my Dad I had started to lose
interest in everything. It was like I was on the outside looking in, and
trying really hard to be on the inside looking out.

"I'm lost, Mom," I said, and started crying. "I don't know what to
do."

"It's that girl, isn't it?"

"I love her, Mom," I cried. "I love her with all that I am."

"It's your first true love," she whispered, pulling me to her. "They
hurt the worse of all of them put together. They're the ones you don't
forget."

"It's not fair," I said.

"Nothing ever is," she said, with a forced smile. "Your Dad's been
acting the same way."

"He has?" I asked.

"Yeah," she said. "Since the day he went down and talked to her father."

"Do you think he knows something?" I asked.

"I can't really say," she replied. "He doesn't talk about it, and he's never home until we're all in bed."

"I wonder what he knows?" I asked.

"Your friend Roy is here," Mom said, changing the subject. "He wanted me to ask if he could visit for a while."

"I guess so," I said. "Give me a moment, and tell him to come in."

"It'll all work out for the best," she said, and kissed me on the cheek. "Just keep the faith, and tomorrow will be a brighter day."

"I don't think I know how to keep the faith," I replied.

"It'll come," she said, and left the room.

"What's up?" Roy said, a few minutes later, as he came into the room.

"I think I'm going insane," I replied.

"You look like shit," he smiled. "You need to start playing your guitar again."

"I have three of them," I said. "I've not bothered to touch one'em in days."

"Maybe now's the time," he said. "You really need to get on with your life."

"I just can't stop thinking about her," I said. "It's everything I do."

"Yeah," Roy said. "And it doesn't help you one bit, does it?"

"No," I said, and picked up one of my guitars. "This is the last thing I wrote."

"Cool," he smiled. "Let's hear it."

"Okay," I said, and started strumming.

> "I never got to say
> What I wanted to say
> I never got . . ."

That was all I could do. The world suddenly came crashing down around me, and I had to escape. To where I had no idea. I just exploded in one screaming rage.

"No," I screamed, and started beating my guitar against the wall, until it exploded as well.

"Take it easy," Roy said, trying to hold me down.

It was of no use. Mom came into the room, just as I broke free of Roy's hold, and pushed past both of them. I ran outside into the rain, and took off on my dirt bike. In the background I could hear both Roy and Mom calling my name. I didn't care. I didn't care about anything. I had finally had enough, and was going to do something about it.

I took a shortcut by using one of the trails we had made that took us to the river faster, and didn't think about the rain. The trail was too slippery for the speed I was going, and caused me to lose control as I was going up one of the hills. I crashed into a group of trees, flew over the handlebars, and landed in a grassy spot about twenty feet away from the crash site.

I was numb, and thought I was dying. The rain had stopped, and I was all alone as lie there unable to move. I closed my eyes, and waited for death to claim me. It was a just reward for the way things had gone.

The only thing that came was sleep.

## CHAPTER FIFTY-FOUR

BY THE TIME I woke up, it had started raining again. I was still lying where I had landed after the crash. No one had come looking for me, so I figured it hadn't been very long ago. More than likely, they just figured I was mad, and needed to cool off.

My bike was totaled. There was no way I was going to be able to fix it anytime soon. This was one of those things that I knew my Dad was just going to love. He'd never let me ride a dirt bike again. Nor would my Mom, once she found out what had happened.

I get all the breaks, when my chips are up.

I looked at my watch; I noticed that it was just about time for Carol Anne to be heading for home. I had enough of this ordeal to last me a lifetime. I was going to find out what the deal was even if it killed me.

Which it almost did.

I waited for Carol Anne, as she made her way home from Jenn's, on the path that I had watched her come and go from every day. Carol Anne would see how desperate I have become, and give into me. If she didn't, I would remind her that we were best friends, and that best friends didn't do each other this way.

"Carol Anne?" I said, stepping out from behind a tree. "I have to talk to you."

"Ryc?" she said, and I noticed tears in her eyes. "You scared the living day lights out of me."

"I didn't mean to," I said.

"What happened to your face?" she asked. "There's a big gash in your forehead, and it's bleeding really bad."

"I wrecked my bike," I said.

"You need to get that taken care of," she said, touching the area of my forehead that hurt like there wasn't a tomorrow. "I'm kind of in a hurry. So what do you want?"

"I need to talk to you," I replied.

"If it's about Jenn," she said. "I promised I wouldn't."

"You have to," I said. "This is tearing me up inside, not knowing from day to day what's really going on."

"Dammit, Ryc," she snapped, and burst into tears. "I promised them I wouldn't tell you. Even if it were the last thing I ever had to do."

"Please," I said, as my own tears started to fall.

"She's dying," Carol Anne said, and I dropped to my knees.

"She's dying?" I repeated, in a question.

This was not at all what I wanted to hear.

"I'm sorry," Carol Anne said, and dropped to her knees beside me. "I wanted to tell you all a long. Your Dad and Mr. Tate didn't think you would be able to deal with it."

"They were right," I said, crying, and looking her in the eyes.

"I know this is really hard," she said, pulling me to her, and wrapping her arms around me. "I wish there were something I could do."

"They wouldn't be able to keep it from me forever," I said. "I'm not that stupid."

"They were going to tell you that Jenn broke it off with you," Carol Anne said. "And that she went back to Canada."

"I'd gone looking for her," I said, pulling away from her, to wipe my eyes.

"That's what I told them," she said.

"What's she dying from?"

"The same kind of cancer that her mother died of," she replied.

"Why isn't she in the hospital?" I asked, getting up to my feet, and helping her up.

"There's nothing they can do," Carol Anne replied. "She's been basically gone for the last two weeks."

"What do you mean?"

"She's in a coma," Carol Anne stated. "They can't figure it out."

"Figure what out?" I asked.

"Why she's still holding on," Carol Anne replied. "That's why I've been going down there every day. Mr. Tate asked me to stay with her, while he made funeral arrangements."

"Is she the one who wanted her to stay in the house?" I asked, starting to form an idea.

"Yes," Carol Anne replied. "She asked her Dad to let her die at home, in the place she loved, and near the one she loved."

"Me?" I choked.

"Yes," Carol Anne said, touching my arm, and bursting into another round of tears. "She told me to tell you that she never stopped loving you. I promised her that I would tell you."

"I know why she's holding on," I said, taking Carol Anne by the shoulders. "She's waiting for me to let her go."

"No," Carol Anne cried, even harder. "She begged us not to let you see her that way."

"That was before she went into the coma," I reminded her. "She didn't want to have to face me with the truth."

"I'm sorry, Ryc," she said, wiping her eyes. "You're probably right. Only I don't think Mr. Tate is going to let you see her."

"He has to sleep sometime," I said.

"No, he doesn't", Carol Anne replied, and shook her head. "He hasn't slept for days. It almost kills him, when he has to leave her."

"I'll get into see her somehow," I said, and took off through the woods toward Jenn's.

"Ryc?" Carol Anne called.

It wasn't any use. My mind was made up. One way or another, I was going to see Jenn. Mostly because I felt that if I didn't do it tonight, I'd never see her alive again, and I didn't want to fail her.

"RYC?" Carol Anne screamed, hoping I would stop.

I turned around briefly, smiled at her, and kept going. I was possessed by the need to do what I knew in my heart Jenn wanted me to do.

It wasn't so much my need anymore, but more hers.

Jenn was calling out to me, and I knew it from the bottom of my heart. I couldn't let her suffer anymore. That's why it was all coming down to the wire. Jenn was ready to go, but she couldn't without saying her unspoken good-bye.

Her heart wouldn't let her go, until I did.

## CHAPTER FIFTY-FIVE

I WENT STRAIGHT TO Jenn's, slipping and falling all the way. When I got there, I took up a perch in the darkest shadows of the woods, so I wouldn't be seen. To my surprise, there was a low light shining in Jenn's room that seemed to be calling me closer and closer.

Mr. Tate was walking around in the living room, like he didn't know what to do. It was the first time I had ever seen him look so lost.

The phone rang, and he walked over to answer it.

"Yes," he said, into the receiver. "No, I haven't seen him as of yet. When I do, I'll tell him that you're worried. Yes, Mr. Lewis, I'll send him home."

He was talking to my Dad.

"All right, all right," Mr. Tate continued to talk. "Yes, and good-bye."

Mr. Tate only smiled, and shook his head.

I made several failed attempts to sneak into the house through the sliding glass door. My goal was to slip into the hallway, which was just off that entrance, and quickly move down it to Jenn's room. Each time I tried, Mr. Tate ended up somewhere where he could spot me, and kept me from my goal.

The phone rang again, and he answered it.

"Hello," he said, then a look of worry flashed across his face. "What is it, Carol Anne? No, I haven't seen Ryc."

There was a short silence.

"She's still hanging on," he said. "Stop crying, Carol Anne. It's not your fault. . . We couldn't keep it from him forever."

There was another pause.

"I don't understand," he said. "What? Are you sure?"

He stopped for a moment, as if he were thinking about what she was saying.

"He actually thinks this?" he asked. "He may be right. Yes, I think she's suffered enough. Don't worry yourself sick about it, Carol Anne."

He stopped to wipe tears from his eyes.

"Please, Carol Anne," he said. "Stop crying. I'll take care of it. You've been a good friend. Jenn was fortunate to have friends like you and Ryc."

He stopped to wipe his eyes again.

"Yes, I will," he said. "Good-bye, Carol Anne."

He hung up the phone, and started down the hallway.

The phone rang again. This time he just stared at it for a long moment, then slowly went over to answer it.

"Hello," he said, with a voice that sounded very tired. "No, Mr. Lewis. I haven't seen him yet. Have the police any news?"

Suddenly, Mr. Tate and I were staring at each other, without even knowing that we were. Yet, for some strange reason I got the feeling that he knew, as surely as I knew. We had made contact with each other.

"If I see him. . ." he said, and hung up the phone.

His attention was fixed on something he could not see. Something outside that was staring back at him from outside the sliding glass door. Slowly, he walked over to the door, and opened it. He looked out briefly, and then walked back into the living room. There he took a seat, and tried to force himself to go to sleep.

I knew he had opened the door for me.

Believing that, I made my way through the door, and down the hall to Jenn's room. I stood outside her door for a long moment, closed my eyes, opened the door, and slowly walked in. All the strength I had given myself to make this journey suddenly came crashing down at my feet. I felt totally helpless.

She was lying silent in her bed. Her eyes were sunken dark into her face, and her skin was a pale white. She looked like a cross between a ghost and a vampire from the soap opera *"Dark Shadows."* This was why she didn't want me to see her. This was why she shut me out of her life, and made me suffer as well.

This was how strong our love was.

"Even in this state," Mr. Tate said, from behind me. "She's still a lovely creature."

"Yes," I choked.

"You should go home," he said, with a hand on my shoulder. "There's nothing you can do for her. Besides, your family is worried sick about you."

"They think I'm going to follow her into death," I whispered, with tears racing down my face. "They just don't get it."

"Is that what you want to do?" he asked, moving over to pull the blankets up around her. "Is that what you think Jenn would want you to do?"

"No," I replied. "She would want me to go on with my life."

"That's right," he said. "She would want you to live for her as well."

"I know," I said, and broke down.

"Stand up, Ryc," he said, coming to my rescue.

"Why?" I cried.

"Don't think about it like that," he said, hugging me close to him. "Think about how much she loved you."

"I am," I said, feeling his tears drop upon my neck, as he held me in his embrace. "It's just not fair for any of us."

"Life never is," he said, pulling away from me, so he could look me in the eyes. "Still we have to live it to the best that we can. Even if it means letting go of someone we love."

"Yeah, I know," I said, and moved over to kneel beside the bed.

"She's in a coma," Mr. Tate said, coming up behind me, and putting his hand back on my shoulder. "She doesn't know we're here."

"She knows," I said, reaching out to take her hand in mine. "I'm the reason why she's still holding on."

"What do you mean?" he asked.

"She wants me to let her go," I said, kind of breaking down again.

"You're a brave man," Mr. Tate said, squeezing my shoulder. "I want to thank you for being what you were to her."

"You've got it wrong, Mr. Tate," I said, fighting the tears that would not stop. "I have to thank you for letting her touch our lives. . . my life with her love."

"You know it's not your fault?" he asked.

"I know it's not," I replied. "I just feel so helpless."

"I know the feeling," he said. "I've sat here night after night wishing I could think of something to change all of this. It's like watching her mother die all over again."

"I'd give my life in trade for hers," I said, brushing the side of her face with my fingers. "That's what she means to me. That's how much I love her."

He didn't reply. There was nothing he could reply to. Once you've said that you loved someone that much, nothing else could ever seem as important.

"I'll love her for the rest of my life," I whispered.

"I know you will, son," he said.

"I'll always love her," I said.

With that spoken, I rose, and kissed her lightly on the lips. That moment etched its self forever in my soul, and would change the way I would allow myself to love in all the years ahead of me.

"I love you, Jennifer," I said, and kissed her again. "I always have, and I always will."

"C'mon," Mr. Tate said, taking me by the shoulders. "You need to go home, and be with your family. They need to know that you're okay."

"Okay," I said, and let him lead me to the door.

"She really did love you, Ryc," he said. "She had the utmost respect for you. She wanted me to let you know how she felt, and I promised her I would."

"Thank you," I said, and stepped out into the night. "If my Dad calls you again, tell him that I'm all right. Tell him that I need to be alone for a while, and that I'll be home shortly."

"I really think you should go home now," Mr. Tate said.

"I can't," I said, turning around to look at him. "I'm all right, Mr. Tate. I just need time to let go."

"I understand," he said, reaching into his pocket. "She wanted you to have this. Carol Anne wrote it for her, just a few hours before she slipped into the coma."

He handed me a sealed envelope.

"The ring inside belonged to my father," he said. "He gave it to her when she was eight years old, and told her to give it to the man she fell in love with. That way it would always stay in the family of the men who loved his women."

"Thanks," I said, and tucked the envelope into my pocket.

"I'll keep you in touch," he said, stepping back into the house.

"Yeah," I whispered, and then disappeared into the shadows.

I went to the Thinking Rock to do my letting go. While setting there, I opened the envelope, and found a gold nugget wedding band, with four diamonds in it. The only finger it would fit on was my right pinky finger. I slid it on, and then opened the letter, which I read by moonlight.

> *Dearest Richart,*
> *I'm sorry I never told you about my illness. I was hoping that it was over, when Daddy and I came back to Tennessee, and you and I would share a long life together. Unfortunately, it didn't go that way. There were so many things I wanted to share with you that time will just not allow. I won't be here when you're reading this. So I'll have to say what I won't ever get to say to you again. I love you, Mr. Richart Drake Lewis. I'll love you for the rest of my life, and beyond. If you're ever lonely, or feeling lost, just think of me, and I'll be there with you in heart.*
> *Forever my love,*
> *Jennifer La'Nette Tate.*

I folded the letter up, and stuck it back into my pocket. That was the hardest moment I have ever known. How do you let go of someone like her, and feel true about anything else? Why was this happening? I kept asking myself. Why couldn't I do anything to save her? What crimes against faith had we committed to cause such a wrath?

"God," I cried up at the heavens. "I would give up my last breath, if it meant she could have one more moment of life."

"Just one more," I whispered.

I waited, but no answer came to me. I was all alone, looking down at the Tennessee River. It swam by me, with no care at all. It already knew where its waters were headed.

"God," I said, climbing to my feet. "Why aren't you listening?"

I still didn't get an answer. Therefore, I couldn't let go of her until I did. Even if it were only a memory tucked safely in my mind. She was all of what love was to me, and all that it ever would be.

Forever true.

# CHAPTER FIFTY-SIX

I WENT HOME TO get my guitar. When I got there, I saw a police car parked in front of the house. Mom must have hit the panic button, and made Dad call the police. Dad was on the front porch talking to the cop.

They just didn't understand that all I needed was some time to myself. Time to think this through, and make some sense of it all. Time was something they needed to take for themselves. Maybe life wouldn't be such a bitch for them if they did.

Figuring it would be better if they didn't know I was there, I climbed through my bedroom window, and went straight for my acoustic guitar. The one I hadn't beaten to death when I took off earlier. I knew I was taking a big chance at getting caught, but it was also the only way I could get my guitar. It had been my best friend for a great number of years, and I knew I could count on it to help me get through this.

Once inside, I heard my Dad giving my little brothers the third degree, and decided to listen. It would be interesting to know just how insane they had gotten with the ordeal. Hearing Dad inside the house told me that either he had come in with the cop, or the cop had left.

That meant I might get a handle on what was going on with the police as well.

"Did you two know about your brother's girlfriend?" Dad asked.

"No," they both said at once.

"We didn't know nothin'," Joe added.

"He never hung out with us," Jim said. "He was always gone somewhere on his motorcycle, or out with his guitar."

"He didn't like us," Joe said. "He said he was too big to play with us."

"Too old," Jim corrected Joe.

I didn't know they thought that way.

"Roy found his dirt bike wreaked on one of the hills," Dad said.

"Was Ryc there?" Mom asked.

"No," said the cop.

He must have come in with Dad.

"I don't want to alarm you," Dad said. "But Roy also found some blood near the accident."

"Oh, God," Mom cried. "He's out there wondering around. Bleeding and God knows what because of all this."

"He'll be all right," Dad said, with a concerned voice.

"I'll tell you why we didn't know about Jennifer," Mom stated.

"Suppose you let me in on it," Dad demanded, in his normal tone.

"You were always too hard on him about that other girl," she said. "He knew how you would react, so he kept her a secret from us."

"I was trying to teach him something about life," Dad said, in defense of his actions. "A boy his age has to know what kind of trouble he can get into by being with a girl."

"He's almost a man," Mom said. "And that's not the way you handled it."

"I did what I thought was right," Dad snapped.

"Calm down, Mr. Lewis," stated the cop. "This isn't going to change things."

"I'll calm down when I know he's okay," Dad yelled. "And then I'll. . ."

"And then you'll what?" asked the cop, cutting him off. "Beat him half to death?"

Dad didn't reply.

"You know they're working on laws that will protect children from abusive parents, don't you?" asked the cop; in a manner that I'm sure was addressed to Dad's behavior.

"What do we do now?" Mom asked, coming to Dad's rescue.

"We'll give him until morning to come home," replied the cop. "If he isn't home by then, we'll call in help to conduct a search of the area."

"But he's not in his right state of mind," Mom said. "What if he does something stupid tonight?"

"Officially," said the cop. "We can't do anything for twenty-four hours. We're a small force, and we believe in serving our community. That's why we're out running the streets and roads now. We really don't want to have to find him hurt or anything."

"You don't know him the way I do," Mom said. "He has too big a heart not to take this lightly."

"Mom?" I questioned, with a whisper.

When did she start paying attention to me? She spent most of her time dodging Dad's wrath, and hiding in the shadows like a forgotten wallflower. A part of me wanted to go in and tell her that I was going to be all right. While the other part knew that I didn't want to face Dad right now. If I'd gone in there, I wouldn't have a chance to be by myself.

"What she's trying to tell you," Dad said. "Is that our son is stupid enough to go out and try to kill himself over this girl."

"Right," I whispered again.

That was my Dad for you. He had all the answers, and knew every thing there was about me. It's also what kept me from going in and letting them know how I was. Neither one of them was right about me. Just because Jenn was going to die, didn't mean that I wanted to die. What would I gain from doing that?

What would Jenn think of me, if I did something like that?

All I needed was a chance to be alone for a while, and deal with this in my own way. Chase my dreams; catch a few, or something stupid like that. I had to learn to deal with it for myself, and that wasn't something they could do for me.

Killing myself was not the answer.

"Let's hope that's not the case," replied the cop, as I crawled back out my window, with my guitar in hand.

Another police car was pulling up, as I ran across the lawn, and almost got caught in his headlight beams. Either he wasn't paying attention, or I was lucky enough to duck out of sight before he saw me.

I wasn't sure what I was going to do at the moment. I really hadn't given myself time enough to think about anything like that. Knowing it was all there inside of my head was how I avoided it the best. There was just too much going on, too fast for anyone to think.

I just knew I couldn't deal with my folks. Especially my Dad, and all the shit he would hit me with. Regrettably, he would only make matters worse than they were. If I were ever to think about killing myself, it would be more like something I'd think about doing, after I had to deal with him.

Believe me, when I say he wasn't what I needed.

## CHAPTER FIFTY-SEVEN

I WENT BACK TO the Thinking Rock to play my guitar, and let it all come together in one big rush. Only I couldn't find anything in my head to play. It was like I had forgotten every thing I knew. In other times when I was upset, playing my guitar was how I was able to deal with the problem.

Not this time.

> "Behind the blade of every knife
> There lives a secret life
> Reaching out to know
> The freedom of a lost soul
> Somewhere down the line . . ."

It didn't sound right, and that in itself made me mad. I wasn't getting anywhere with it. In an outburst, I smacked my guitar really hard, and through it into the bushes.

Jenn wouldn't leave my thoughts.

It was starting to get to me the way I didn't want it to.

"Ryc?" Carol Anne asked, walking up from behind me.

"Hey," I whispered.

"Are you all right?"

"I've lost it," I said, turning around to face her.

I was crying.

"Oh, Ryc," she said, cradling my head to her chest. "It'll come back in due time. Just give it some time to heal."

"It's harder than I thought it was gonna be," I confessed.

"It always is," she said, still holding me close to her.

"How did you know I'd be here?"

"I know you," she whispered, and kissed the top of my head. "You know the police are out looking for you, don't you?"

"Yeah," I said. "I saw them at the house."

"I see," she said.

"You're going to get killed for being out so late, you know," I said, looking up into her eyes. "You're crying."

"So are you," she reminded me. "By the way, my Dad knows I'm out looking for you."

"Good excuse," I smiled.

"It's not an excuse," she said, and changed the subject. "Have you heard how Jenn is?"

"She wasn't doing too good when I saw her last," I replied. "I really don't think she's gonna be with us much longer."

"You saw her?"

"Right after you called Mr. Tate," I said. "He opened the door, and let me come in."

"Then you really know what the real deal is," she said.

"Yeah," I said, and stood up to get my guitar.

"I'm sorry, Ryc," Carol Anne said, making no effort to hide her tears that shined in the moonlight like trails of blood. "I know how you feel about her."

"I know you do," I agreed.

"I've got some bad news for you," she said. "My father is sending me to my aunts for the school year."

"Why?" I asked.

"He thinks it would be best if I weren't around to get caught up in the aftermath of all of this," she replied.

"How do you feel about it?"

"I think he might be right," she said. "But I think I can't get caught up in it any more than I already am."

"Yeah," I said, because I didn't know what else to say.

"What are you going to do?"

"My folks think I'm gonna kill myself," I said.

"Are you?" she asked, and I could tell she was serious.

"No," I smiled. "That wouldn't solve anything. Besides, Jenn wouldn't want me to do something like that, and I wouldn't be around for you to pick on."

"I won't be around," she reminded me.

"Yeah," I said. "You won't, will ya?"

"Just the same," she said. "I kind of understand how your parents might think that you could do something like that."

"I'll admit that it's kind of crossed my mind," I said. "Only I feel like I'll die without her in my life, but that doesn't mean I want to die."

"Good," she said.

"First love is forever love," I said. "I'll always remember that she was mine."

"That's why I can't love you that way anymore," Carol Anne said. "I'm not Jenn, and I don't want to try to replace her."

"It's okay," I said. "I understand."

"No, you don't," she said, and burst into tears. "I love you, Ryc. I love you so much it hurts. I would have given anything in the world to get you to love me, but not this. I'm your friend, Ryc. That's all that I can be."

"I know," I said. "I'm not asking you for anything."

"Shut up," she said, and pushed me. "I have to get this all out now, or I never will."

"Okay," I said, surprised at the way she was acting.

"If you and I were to get together after this," she said. "I to would remember that Jenn was your first love, and that would always remind me that I only stood in the shadow of what she was to you."

"So none of us win," I said.

"As friends we do," she said. "As lovers, we would only end up resenting each other for the way we became lovers, and Jenn would be there to remind us again. It would be like we were betraying her in some way."

"Why are you bringing this up?"

"Because I've been thinking about it a lot lately," she said. "I've decided that I would much rather be your friend, then take a chance on losing what we share to love."

"I can deal with that," I said. "It's what I've been fighting all a long."

"I know," she said, with a soft smile. "I need to get back to the house before they start looking for me. Your Dad would probably think we were running off together."

"Knowing him," I smiled. "He probably already does."

"You're gonna be okay, right?"

"I'm gonna be okay," I said.

"Good," she said, and started backing away.

"Do me a favor, will ya?"

"Anything," she said.

"Don't tell 'em you found me," I said.

"I won't," she smiled.

"Carol Anne?" I asked just to say her name.

"What?" she asked, stepping back up to where I was.

"Always," I said, and kissed her on the lips.

"Always," she repeated, and returned the kiss.

"I'll always be your friend," I said, holding her in my arms. "And I'll always love you, no matter how far time drifts us a part."

"I know," she said, pulling away from me, and headed for home.

It was going to be a long, long night.

If the police were going to start looking for me really hard come morning, I needed to get out of there as fast as I could. I didn't really want to leave Jenn, but then I didn't want to see her dead either. That would make it all so final, and I couldn't let that happen. As long as I could think that she might be alive somewhere, she would be alive in my heart. Waiting for the day we could meet once more, and share our love.

There really was nothing I could do, and I couldn't say good-bye. Seeing her dead would be the same as saying good-bye, and I couldn't do that.

Not with her.

Not with Jenn.

Instead, I was leaving in search of my destiny.

I knew they would probably think that I had gone to Nashville, because that was the capital of the music world. It would be the most logical place for me to head. Only I was smarter than that. I was headed for Memphis, the rock and roll capital of the world.

If Elvis could make it there, so could I.

Okay, I know I'm not thinking this all the way out. It's just something I've got to do. Something I can't face. The world has robbed me of more than I should ever have to give up at my age. So I'm going to take a portion of it back.

All I had left was my music. My soul was in the care of the man upstairs, and my heart was lying with a beautiful young lady in a house on the Tennessee River. A beautiful young lady that I loved more than anything, and who I would never be able to see again.

My mind was made up.

# CHAPTER FIFTY-EIGHT

THE STATE POLICE PICKED me up somewhere around ten in the morning, walking down Interstate 40. When they pulled up behind me, I turned around, and walked back to their car. There was no way I could out run them, so I figured I'd better give up my quest for now. Besides, my legs were starting to get really tired.

They radioed in that they had picked me up, and were in route to my parent's house. I had to direct them on the back roads, because they didn't know them. Woodland Shores is one way in, and one way out. I wondered silently if they would be able to figure it out.

"Where were you headed?" asked the driver.

"Nowhere," I replied.

"Carrying that guitar," said the other cop. "I bet you were headed to Memphis. Think you're gonna be the next Elvis?"

"Give me a break?" I asked.

"You are getting a break," said the driver." Normally, we take you runaways to jail. As a favor to the Decatur County Sheriff's Office, we're taking you home to face your parents."

"I'd rather go to jail," I stated, realizing how my Dad was going to react.

They both laughed at me, as if it were some kind of joke. To me it wasn't a joke. I knew better. To me it was the end of my life.

Mom was standing in the doorway, when we pulled up into the drive. My brothers were in the side yard, and Dad had his head stuck under the hood of his truck. That's what he did, when he needed to work something out for himself, and wasn't sure what to do.

"Wait here," said the driver, as he climbed out of the car.

"This is it, kid," said the other cop. "This is where it all comes to head."

"Don't remind me," I said.

"Jim?" Mom called, as she walked out onto the porch.

"Mr. Lewis?" asked the cop, as Dad walked up to him, wiping off his hands with a shop rag he always kept in his back pocket. "I think we have your son in the car."

"That's him," Dad said, bending down to look at me.

"Do you want us to take him in as a runaway?" asked the cop. "Or would you like to take charge of him?"

"I'll take him," Dad said, as the cop went back to open the car door.

"Dad?" I asked scared to death that he was going to kill me.

"I'm sorry, Ryc," he said, and I knew what he was telling me.

"She's gone, isn't she?" I asked, as tears started racing down my cheeks.

This was truly where it all came to head.

"Yes," he replied, staring at me in away I've never known him to. "She passed away last night, shortly after you left her."

He didn't have to tell me. It was something I already knew.

"I loved her, Dad," I cried, and dropped to my knees.

"I know you did, son," he said, kneeling in front of me, as a tear ran down the side of his face.

It was the first time I had ever seen him cry.

"It's not fair," I mumbled.

"I know it's hard," he said, with his hands on my shoulders. "But you're a braver man than I. . . I've never had to face anything like this."

"What do I do?"

"Live," he said. "Keep her alive inside of you, and she'll never really be gone."

"With every breath," I said, and broke down completely.

He did something in that moment that he had not done since I was a very small boy. He took me into his open arms, and let me cry.

## THE END?

## ABOUT THE AUTHOR

Richart Drake Lewis was born in the back seat of a '53 Chevy on the 23$^{rd}$ birthday of Elvis Presley in front of Oscar Gibson's General Store in Jeannette, Tennessee. He was raised in Central Indiana where he currently resides.

He graduated from Tipton High School (Tipton, Indiana) in 1978, and joined the United States Army that same year. He attended college at Austin Peavy University, graduated with three writing diplomas from ICL, one diploma from NRI at McGraw Hill, and received an OJT diploma in Field Journalism for his work in the Special Forces as a Recon Expert and CID operative.

Over the years he's performed with the bands Satin's Lot, KOT (Knights of Terror), Hereafter, and Darkangel. He also won several awards performing as Elvis Presley, Buddy Holly, Roy Orbison, Conway Twitty, and Ricky Nelson. He has recorded several cover songs on CD, and is currently working on a gospel CD of some his Christian material with his church. The first song off that proposed CD (Don't You Know) has been well received, and is preformed regularly in services.

He has had poetry published in several poetry anthologies between the years 1995 and 2001, has written for three different newspapers where he won two writing awards, and has had his own column in two newsletter's titled "Ryc's Place". He has one book of lyric poetry (Rock and Roll Dreams) published by Northland Publications in 1992, and a book of poetry and pictures (Return to Me) published by Recollections, Inc. in 2000. "Down a

Road I've Never Been" is his first novel, and the first in a series of seven novels based upon the time period.

As an artist he has a color pencil drawing of General John Tipton hanging in the Tipton County Public Library's Indiana Room where it's been hanging for the last 21 years, an ink drawing of James Dean in the Fairmount Historical Museum, a color pencil drawing in the Association of Retarded Citizens, a color pencil drawing in the Sheridan Healthcare Center, and recently an oil painting of General John Tipton hanging in the Tipton County Historical Center. He also illustrated the cover of "Down a Road I've Never Been" in color pencil.

He has been married three times, has three sons (Shawnric Ryan, James Byron Dean, and Glen Michael Leland) with his second wife. At the moment he is single and has no intention in getting married anytime in the future. "The next thirty years belong to me and my sons," he reported on the subject.

He currently resides in Tipton, Indiana next door to his mother, and maintains a close relationship to his friends and family in Decatur County Tennessee.

Printed in the United States
15972LVS00001B/475-492